AF238485

# Awakening Shadows

## The Astral Chronicles, Volume 1

### ANANT RAM BOSS

Published by ANANT RAM, 2023.

This is a work of fiction. Similarities to real people, places, or events are entirely coincidental.

AWAKENING SHADOWS

**First edition. December 21, 2023.**

ISBN: 979-8223691891

Written by ANANT RAM BOSS.

# Also by ANANT RAM BOSS

**1**
The Chronicles of Alarion -Part-6 "Alarion and the Nexus of Netheron"
"The Chronicles of Alarion -Part-7-"Alarion and the Legacy of Luminarya"

**The Astral Chronicles**
Awakening Shadows
Awakening Shadows

**Standalone**
Love's Delectable Harmony

# Table of Contents

"The Astral Chronicles" is a journey that transcends time and space, offering readers a unique blend of cultural richness, mythical encounters, and a narrative that explores the interconnectedness of the physical and astral dimensions. With each book, the series unfolds like a tapestry, weaving together threads of destiny, magic, and the enduring spirit of India.

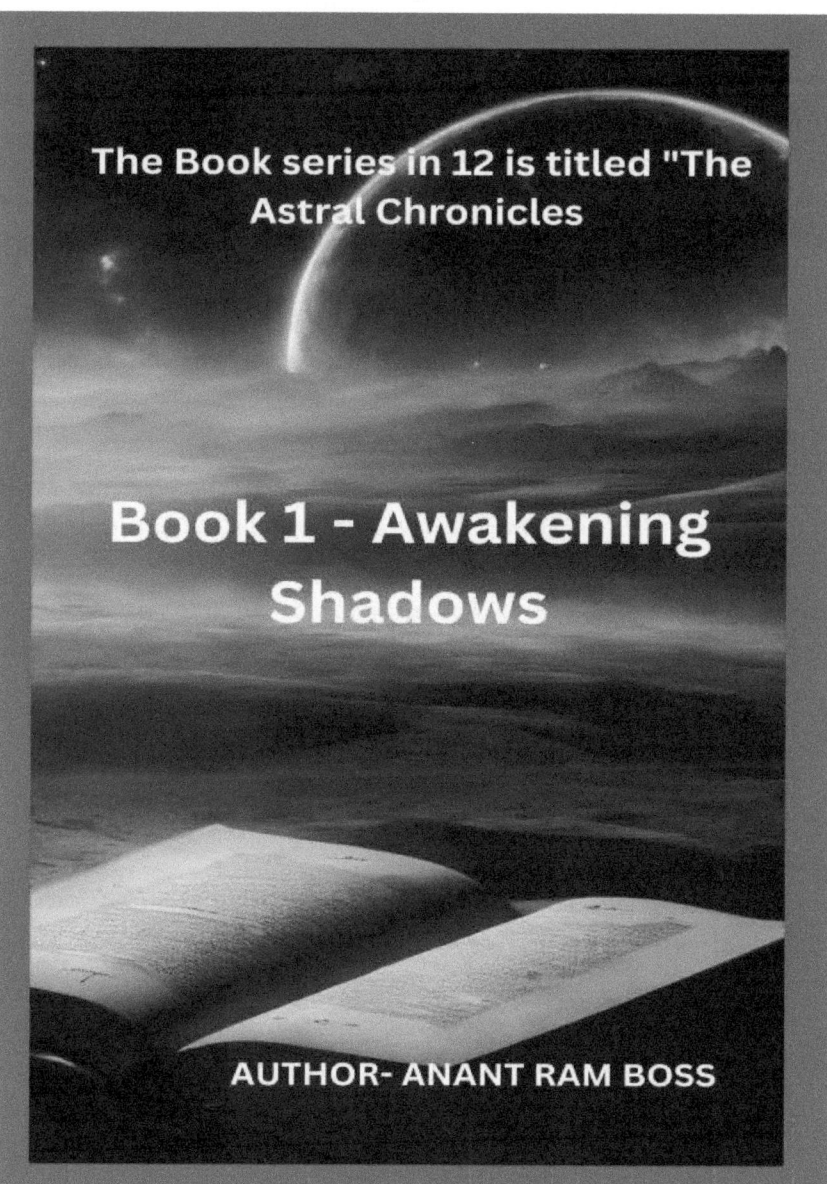

The Book series in 12 titled "The Astral Chronicles: Book 1 - Awakening Shadows"

*Overview of "The Astral Chronicles" Series:*

*"The Astral Chronicles" is a sweeping 12-book epic that delves into the intersection of ancient mysticism, modern intrigue, and the rich cultural tapestry of India, this series transports readers into a world where the boundaries between the physical and astral realms blur, revealing hidden truths and cosmic prophecies.*

*Setting: The series unfolds against the backdrop of diverse Indian landscapes, from the mystical Ghats of Varanasi to the forgotten ruins of Hampi, the serene Spiti Valley, and the spiritual haven of Rishikesh. Each setting is meticulously woven into the narrative, serving as a gateway to ancient secrets and mystical encounters.*

*Characters: At the heart of "The Astral Chronicles" are three protagonists: Aditya "Aadi" Sharma, a charismatic archaeologist; Priya Mehta, a brilliant astrophysicist; and Rajveer "Raj" Kapoor, a skilled martial artist. As they unite forces, the trio embarks on a quest to decipher celestial prophecies, unravel ancient mysteries, and confront both terrestrial and astral adversaries.*

*Plot Progression:*

*Books 1-4: Aadi's discovery of an ancient artifact in Varanasi triggers the awakening of dormant powers, leading to the formation of the trio.*

*Celestial prophecies draw them to Hampi, where they delve into the forgotten empire's secrets and initiate their journey into astral realms.*

*Spiritual training in Rishikesh strengthens their abilities and bonds, setting the stage for the challenges ahead.*

*Books 5-8: Portals across India unveil encounters with mythical beings and ancient deities, testing the protagonists' resolve.*

*Hampi's ruins become a battleground as the team grapples with an impending cosmic imbalance and ancient evils in Varanasi resurface.*

*The characters confront personal histories and ancestral ties, unveiling connections to celestial entities and the true purpose of their quest.*

*Books 9-12: Mystic alliances are forged as the protagonists face challenges requiring cooperation with mortal and astral beings.*

*A climactic revelation leads the team to a mystical nexus point, blurring the boundaries between the physical and astral realms.*

*The series crescendos with the ultimate challenge in "Eclipse of Eternity," where sacrifices are made to restore harmony and prevent the unraveling of existence.*

*"Beyond the Veil" serves as the epic conclusion, as Aadi, Priya, and Raj navigate the astral realms and ensure a balanced coexistence between mortal and astral worlds.*

*Visual Style: "The Astral Chronicles" incorporates cinematic elements, including high-octane action sequences, breathtaking shots of Indian landscapes, and a soundtrack blending traditional and contemporary music. The visual style enhances the immersive experience, bringing to life the enchanting fusion of ancient mysticism and contemporary storytelling.*

*"The Astral Chronicles" is a journey that transcends time and space, offering readers a unique blend of cultural richness, mythical encounters, and a narrative that explores the interconnectedness of the physical and astral dimensions. With each book, the series unfolds like a tapestry, weaving together threads of destiny, magic, and the enduring spirit of India.*

*Book 1: "Awakening Shadows" Introduces Aditya "Aadi" Sharma, a charismatic archaeologist, as he discovers an ancient artifact in Varanasi that awakens dormant mystical powers.*

*Book 2: "Celestial Convergence" Aadi joins forces with astrophysicist Priya Mehta and martial artist Rajveer "Raj" Kapoor to decode celestial prophecies in Hampi.*

*Book 3: "Whispers of the Himalayas" The trio ventures into Spiti Valley to unravel the secrets guarded by ancient monasteries and learn the art of astral travel.*

*Book 4: "Riddles of Rishikesh" In Rishikesh, the protagonists undergo spiritual training and confront personal challenges, strengthening their bonds and abilities.*

*Book 5: "Portals of the Past" The team discovers portals scattered across India, leading to encounters with mythical creatures and ancient deities.*

*Book 6: "Echoes from Vijayanagara" Hampi's forgotten empire holds the key to an impending cosmic imbalance, and the protagonists must navigate its ruins to prevent catastrophe.*

*Book 7: "Veil of Varanasi" Varanasi becomes a battleground as ancient evils resurface, testing the limits of the protagonists' powers.*

*Book 8: "Threads of Fate" The characters delve into their ancestral histories, uncovering connections to celestial beings and the true purpose of their journey.*

*Book 9: "Mystic Alliances" Allies and enemies emerge as the characters face challenges that require alliances with both mortal and astral entities.*

*Book 10: "The Astral Nexus" A climactic revelation leads the team to a mystical nexus point, where the boundaries between the physical and astral realms blur.*

*Book 11: "Eclipse of Eternity" The cosmic imbalance reaches its peak, and the protagonists must make sacrifices to restore harmony and prevent the unraveling of existence.*

*Book 12: "Beyond the Veil" The epic conclusion sees Aadi, Priya, and Raj facing the ultimate challenge, navigating the astral realms, and ensuring a balanced coexistence between the mortal and astral worlds.*

*Visual Style: Cinematic sequences feature high-octane action, breathtaking shots of Indian landscapes, and a soundtrack that blends traditional and contemporary music to enhance the cultural atmosphere.*

*"The Astral Chronicles" takes readers on a transformative journey, blending ancient mysticism with modern-day challenges, and weaving a tapestry of cultural richness that mirrors the diverse and enchanting landscapes of India.*

## Introduction to "The Astral Chronicles: Book 1 - Awakening Shadows"

In the heart of Varanasi, where the Ganges River whispers ancient secrets and the sacred Ghats echo with the footsteps of pilgrims, a charismatic archaeologist named Aditya "Aadi" Sharma embarks on a journey that will unravel the very fabric of reality. "The Astral Chronicles: Awakening Shadows" introduces readers to a world where the mystical and the mundane collide, and the past holds the key to a cosmic awakening.

Chapter by chapter, we follow Aadi's footsteps as he unearths an ancient artifact along the banks of the Ganges, setting in motion a chain of events that will awaken dormant powers within him. The artifact, adorned with enigmatic symbols, possesses a mysterious energy that transcends the boundaries of time and space.

As Aadi delves into the shadows of Varanasi, he begins to experience vivid dreams that draw him into the astral plane. Celestial whispers and visions of ancient deities beckon him toward a destiny intertwined with the very fabric of the universe. With each passing chapter, the veil between the physical and astral realms grows thinner, revealing a world steeped in mysticism and untold power.

Joined by Priya Mehta, a brilliant astrophysicist with a fascination for celestial anomalies, and Rajveer "Raj" Kapoor, a skilled martial artist with a connection to ancient guardians, Aadi forms an unlikely alliance. Together, they embark on a journey to Hampi, the forgotten empire, where the ruins conceal secrets that echo through the corridors of time.

Amidst the ruins of Hampi, the trio faces celestial convergence, astral echoes, and trials that test the limits of their newfound abilities. The narrative unfolds against the backdrop of rich Indian landscapes, from the spiritual haven of Rishikesh to the mystical alleys of Varanasi, as the team undergoes spiritual training to navigate the astral realms consciously.

The introduction sets the stage for a gripping tale of self-discovery, celestial prophecies, and a looming cosmic imbalance. As Aadi's connection to the ancient artifact deepens, shadows stir, and a dark force from the astral plane threatens to unravel the very fabric of existence.

Join Aadi, Priya, and Raj on a journey where each chapter unravels layers of ancient mysteries, forging bonds that transcend time, and propelling them towards a destiny that will shape the fate of mortal and astral realms alike. "Awakening Shadows" is the inaugural chapter of "The Astral Chronicles," a series that weaves together the threads of Indian mysticism, cultural richness, and a quest that transcends the boundaries of reality itself.

# Description

Step into the enchanting city of Varanasi, where the mystical energies of the Ganges River and the ageless Ghats set the stage for an extraordinary journey. "The Astral Chronicles: Awakening Shadows" beckons readers into a world where ancient artifacts and celestial prophecies converge, introducing Aditya "Aadi" Sharma, a charismatic archaeologist with an insatiable curiosity for the unknown.

As Aadi unearths an ancient artifact along the sacred Ghats, its dormant powers trigger a series of events that will propel him into the heart of ancient mysteries. The artifact, adorned with enigmatic symbols, becomes a vessel for the astral energies that lie dormant within Varanasi's spiritual tapestry.

The narrative unfolds with each chapter as Aadi, accompanied by the brilliant astrophysicist Priya Mehta and the skilled martial artist Rajveer "Raj" Kapoor, embarks on a journey to Hampi, the forgotten empire. Through vivid storytelling, readers traverse mystical ruins, decoding celestial patterns, and confronting astral echoes that blur the boundaries between reality and the unseen realms.

The journey extends to Rishikesh, a spiritual haven nestled at the foothills of the Himalayas, where the trio undergoes spiritual training. The characters' bonds deepen amidst the serenity of Rishikesh, preparing them for the astral trials that wait.

"Awakening Shadows" invites readers to witness Aadi's transformation as he navigates the astral plane, fueled by dreams that unravel the secrets of ancient deities. With celestial convergence on the horizon, the team grapples with their newfound abilities, uncovering a cosmic imbalance that threatens the delicate equilibrium between the mortal and astral worlds.

As the characters return to Varanasi, shadows stir, and the ancient evils lurking in the astral plane awaken. Mira Devi, a mysterious guardian, appears, revealing prophecies that intertwine the destinies of the trio. The climax in Varanasi becomes a battleground where the team must confront not only external threats but also the shadows within themselves.

"Awakening Shadows" sets the stage for "The Astral Chronicles," a 12-book series that promises an immersive blend of Indian mysticism, celestial intrigue, and the enduring spirit of adventure. Richly detailed landscapes, intricate characters, and a narrative that seamlessly weaves together ancient prophecies and contemporary challenges make this book a captivating introduction to a series that transcends the boundaries of reality. Prepare to embark on a journey where the shadows of the past awaken, and destinies are forged amidst the cosmic dance of the astral realms.

## About the Author: Anant Ram Boss

Anant Ram Boss is an accomplished author with a passion for creating immersive worlds and captivating stories. His journey into the realm of writing began at an early age when he discovered the magic of words and the power of storytelling. Anant Ram's dedication to his craft and his relentless pursuit of literary excellence has made him a notable figure in the world of fantasy literature.

With an imaginative mind that knows no bounds, Anant Ram has the ability to transport readers to enchanting and mysterious realms. His writing is known for its vivid descriptions, well-drawn characters, and intricate plots that keep readers eagerly turning pages. He has an innate talent for weaving intricate tales filled with magic, adventure, and profound themes.

Throughout his career, Anant Ram has received acclaim for his ability to craft epic sagas and captivating series that resonate with readers of all ages, as the books series has garnered a devoted following, and it showcases Anant Ram's mastery of the fantasy genre.

When he's not lost in the worlds he creates, Anant Ram enjoys exploring the great outdoors, indulging in his love for photography, and seeking inspiration from the beauty of the natural world. His appreciation for nature often finds its way into his storytelling, enriching his narratives with a deep connection to the environment and the magic that exists within it.

Anant Ram Boss is not only a storyteller but also a world-builder, a dreamer, and an explorer of the human experience through the lens of fantasy literature. With each new book he writes, he invites readers to embark on journeys of the imagination, fostering a love for the magical and the wondrous that resides within us all.

# Chapter 1: The Sacred Ghats of Varanasi

**Introduce Varanasi's mystical ambiance.**
**Aadi begins an excavation project along the Ganges.**

Varanasi, the ancient city where time seemed to dance on the riverbanks of the Ganges, held secrets woven into the very fabric of its mystical ambiance. As the sun dipped below the horizon, casting a golden glow upon the labyrinthine alleys and the towering Ghats, a sense of divinity permeated the air. It was within this sacred haven that Aditya "Aadi" Sharma, a charismatic archaeologist with a passion for unearthing the past, found himself drawn into a journey that would defy the boundaries of both history and reality.

Aadi stood on the edge of the Ghats, the soft murmur of the Ganges mingling with the distant sounds of temple bells and the hushed whispers of pilgrims. The air was thick with the scent of incense, carrying with it the weight of centuries-old stories and spiritual fervor. Aadi, a tall figure with an unruly mop of dark hair, gazed across the sacred river, feeling the pull of ancient energies that resonated within the very stones beneath his feet.

With an eager glint in his eyes, Aadi set his sights on an excavation project that promised to unearth the mysteries buried beneath layers of time. The dig site, marked by weathered pillars and the remnants of a forgotten era, lay along the Ganges, where the convergence of earthly and divine energies was palpable. As the city of Varanasi held its breath in the embrace of the night, Aadi's team began the meticulous process of uncovering the secrets that had slept for centuries.

The first shovelful of earth revealed fragments of pottery adorned with faded patterns, a testament to the artisans of an era long past. Aadi, fueled by the thrill of discovery, guided his team with an unwavering determination. The Ganges, reflecting the luminous glow of the moon, seemed to bear witness to the unfolding excavation as if acknowledging the significance of what lay beneath the surface.

As the night deepened, the excavation site revealed more than pottery and ancient bricks. Aadi's hands, calloused from years of digging through history, brushed against something cold and smooth. His fingers traced the contours of an object buried in the earth, and when he unearthed it, a gasp escaped his lips.

In the pale moonlight, Aadi held an artifact aloft, its surface adorned with symbols that seemed to pulse with otherworldly energy. The artifact, resonating with the very heartbeat of Varanasi, emitted a faint, ethereal glow. It was a discovery that would mark the beginning of a journey beyond the realms of conventional understanding.

Little did Aadi know that in unearthing this ancient artifact along the sacred Ghats of Varanasi, he had opened a gateway to a world where shadows danced with the divine, and the past beckoned to shape the future? The mystic ambiance of Varanasi had bestowed upon him a key—a key that would awaken dormant mystical powers and set in motion the unfolding saga of "The Astral Chronicles."

# Chapter 2: Unearthing the Artifact

**Aadi stumbles upon an ancient artifact with unknown symbols. The artifact emits a mysterious energy.**

In the hushed night along the sacred Ghats of Varanasi, Aditya "Aadi" Sharma's excavation team worked diligently, their tools slicing through layers of time and history. The air was thick with anticipation, charged with the essence of the ancient city. As Aadi directed the excavation, the moon cast a silvery glow upon the river, revealing secrets that lay dormant for centuries.

Aadi, his eyes keen and curious, was drawn to a particular spot. The earth beneath his shovel felt different as if it held a secret waiting to be uncovered. With every careful dig, the soil gave way to something solid. Aadi's hands brushed against a cold, smooth surface, and he instinctively knew this was no ordinary find.

As the team gathered around, their faces illuminated by lantern light, Aadi carefully unearthed the object. It was an artifact unlike anything seen before in the ancient city. Its surface was etched with symbols that seemed to dance with an arcane energy—a language forgotten by time, yet pulsating with a mysterious power.

The artifact, cradled in Aadi's hands, emitted a soft, ethereal glow, casting intricate shadows on the surrounding stones. The symbols, though unfamiliar, resonated with an otherworldly beauty that captured the attention of the entire excavation team. The air itself seemed to vibrate with ancient energy as if the artifact held the very breath of Varanasi's spiritual past.

Aadi, captivated by the unearthly radiance, felt a subtle current passing through his fingers as they traced the symbols. It was a sensation, a connection to something beyond the realms of human comprehension. The artifact seemed to respond to Aadi's touch as if acknowledging the archaeologist as its custodian.

As the team watched in awe, a subtle hum emanated from the artifact—a harmonious blend of mystical resonance. The air crackled with an intangible force, and the surroundings seemed to blur, momentarily transcending the boundaries of the physical world. Varanasi, with its ancient Ghats and timeless river, became a backdrop to a moment where the veil between the ordinary and the extraordinary grew thin.

The discovery of the artifact marked a turning point, not just in Aadi's life but in the very fabric of reality. The mysterious energy that emanated from the artifact hinted at a power waiting to be unraveled—a key to unlocking the secrets of the universe. As the night unfolded along the sacred Ghats of Varanasi, Aadi held in his hands a bridge between the forgotten past and the uncharted territories of the future, setting the stage for a journey that would transcend the boundaries of time and space—the journey of "The Astral Chronicles."

# Chapter 3: Nightfall Revelation

**Aadi experiences a vivid dream revealing glimpses of ancient deities.**
**The artifact's power starts affecting Aadi's dreams.**

The night in Varanasi unfolded like a tapestry of shadows and whispers, with the ancient artifact cradled in Aadi's hands casting a subtle glow upon the sacred Ghats. As the city slept, Aadi found himself succumbing to a restless slumber, his consciousness drawn into the depths of the mystical dreamscape.

In the realm between wakefulness and the ethereal unknown, Aadi witnessed a vivid dreamscape that transcended the boundaries of time. Ancient deities, adorned in celestial splendor, danced across the cosmic tapestry. Their forms were luminescent, with eyes that held the wisdom of epochs and voices that echoed through the corridors of eternity.

Glimpses of a bygone era unfolded before Aadi's dreaming eyes—a time when gods and mortals coexisted in harmonious balance. A celestial dance, accompanied by the melodic hum of the universe, painted a portrait of a world where the boundaries between the earthly and the divine were fluid and interconnected.

Aadi, a mere observer in this astral ballet, felt the resonance of the artifact within the dream. The symbols carved upon its surface manifested as shimmering constellations, aligning with the movements of the celestial beings. It was as though the artifact was a conduit, a bridge that linked the dreamscape to the tangible reality of Varanasi.

As the dream unfolded, Aadi found himself standing before an ancient deity—a figure of ethereal grace and cosmic power. The deity's eyes, pools of infinite wisdom, met Aadi's gaze with a knowing familiarity. Unspoken words echoed through the astral realm, revealing glimpses of a destiny entwined with the very fabric of the universe.

Awakening from the dream, Aadi found himself back along the sacred Ghats, the echoes of celestial melodies still resonating in his mind. The artifact, now nestled in his pocket, seemed to hum with an otherworldly energy that lingered from the dream. It was as if the astral plane and the waking world had briefly merged, leaving an indelible imprint upon Aadi's soul.

Night after night, Aadi's dreams became a canvas painted with the vibrant hues of ancient narratives. The deities whispered secrets of the cosmos, their cryptic messages intertwining with the artifact's enigmatic energy. Aadi, now both archaeologist and dreamer, found himself on a precipice between two worlds, each revelation deepening the mystery that unfolded in the heart of Varanasi.

The artifact's power, no longer confined to the waking hours, began to shape the very fabric of Aadi's dreams. As the lines between reality and the astral realm blurred, a cosmic dance of destiny and discovery commenced—a dance set against the mystical backdrop of Varanasi, where the ancient city itself seemed to hold the keys to secrets that transcended the confines of time. The artifact, a silent witness to the revelations in the night, beckoned Aadi deeper into the labyrinth of the unknown—a journey that would unravel the threads of "The Astral Chronicles."

# Chapter 4: The Call of the Astral

**Aadi feels an inexplicable pull towards the astral plane.**
**Mysterious occurrences intensify around Varanasi.**

Varanasi, steeped in the mystique of centuries, began to unveil its secrets with an ethereal allure that wrapped around Aditya "Aadi" Sharma like an invisible current. The artifact, now a conduit to ancient realms, had woven a bridge between Aadi's waking hours and the dreamscape where celestial beings danced. As each night passed, the call of the astral plane grew stronger, pulling Aadi towards an inexplicable journey beyond the tangible.

In the waking world, Aadi found himself drawn to the Ghats with an irresistible force. The ancient stones beneath his feet seemed to hum with vibrations that resonated in harmony with the artifact nestled in his pocket. A sense of anticipation hung in the air, as if Varanasi itself waited the unfolding of a cosmic tale.

The Ghats, bathed in the soft glow of dawn, became a stage for mysterious occurrences. Shadows moved with a life of their own, mirroring the unseen dance of the astral plane. Aadi, attuned to the rhythms of the ancient city, felt the very air shimmer with an energy that transcended the ordinary.

As Aadi stood along the riverbank, the artifact pulsed with a rhythmic beat, responding to the call of the astral. He closed his eyes, allowing the pull to guide him into a state of meditation. In the silent depths of his mind, the symbols on the artifact transformed into gateways, inviting him to step beyond the veil of reality.

The first time Aadi consciously entered the astral plane, the world around him became a kaleidoscope of vibrant colors and ethereal landscapes. Celestial beings, mirroring the deities from his dreams, welcomed him with an otherworldly grace. The boundaries between the earthly and the divine dissolved, leaving Aadi suspended in the cosmic dance of the astral realms.

Yet, with each astral journey, the mysterious occurrences in Varanasi intensified. The river whispered ancient hymns, and the wind carried cryptic messages. Residents spoke of inexplicable phenomena—shadows taking form, celestial whispers in the night, and a subtle hum that seemed to emanate from the very stones that lined the sacred Ghats.

Aadi, now a conduit between the physical and astral, became a harbinger of change in Varanasi. His astral experiences left imprints upon the city, leaving behind a trail of mystical energy that intertwined with the very essence of the ancient streets. Those who crossed his path felt the subtle shifts as if the boundaries between the tangible and the unseen were thinning.

The artifact, once a dormant relic, now pulsed with life, mirroring the heartbeat of the astral plane. Aadi, with each astral sojourn, delved deeper into the mysteries that unfolded around him. The call of the astral, an irresistible force, echoed through the ancient city, promising revelations that transcended the limits of human understanding.

Varanasi, now a canvas painted with the strokes of the astral dance, held its breath in anticipation of the cosmic tale that Aadi was destined to unravel. The city, with its labyrinthine alleys and timeless Ghats, became a stage where the call of the astral intertwined with the echoes of the past, setting the stage for the next chapter in "The Astral Chronicles."

# Chapter 5: Encounter at the Ghats

**Aadi meets a mysterious figure by the Ganges who hints at the
artifact's significance.**
**The figure disappears, leaving Aadi intrigued.**

The sacred Ghats of Varanasi bathed in the soft glow of moonlight,
held the secrets of centuries within their ancient stones. As
Aditya "Aadi" Sharma continued to be drawn into the cosmic dance of
the astral, he found himself once again standing along the riverbank,
the artifact resonating with the rhythm of the unseen realms.

The night was alive with mystical energies, and Aadi's senses were
heightened as he surveyed the Ghats. Suddenly, a mysterious figure
materialized from the shadows—a silhouette woven with the essence
of the astral. The air shimmered as the figure approached, and Aadi felt
the weight of an ancient presence.

The enigmatic figure, clad in flowing robes that seemed to mirror
the celestial constellations, spoke in a voice that echoed with the
wisdom of ages. "Aditya Sharma, seeker of the astral realms," the figure
intoned, their eyes reflecting the ethereal glow of the artifact. "The key
you hold is more than a relic; it is a bridge between the realms, a thread
that weaves through the cosmic tapestry."

Aadi, both awestruck and intrigued, felt a resonance with the
figure's words. Questions swirled in his mind, seeking answers to the
mysteries that unfolded around him. The figure extended a hand,
gesturing toward the artifact that Aadi held. "In your hands lies a
fragment of a forgotten cosmic design. The symbols etched upon it

carry the echoes of a celestial language, a language you are destined to decipher."

As the figure spoke, the symbols on the artifact seemed to come alive, shifting and rearranging in response to the cosmic energy that enveloped them. Aadi, entranced by the unfolding spectacle, sensed the weight of a cosmic responsibility settling upon his shoulders.

"Varanasi," continued the figure, "has been a crucible of ancient energies, and you, Aditya, are the chosen one—the bridge between the earthly and the astral. The artifact is a key to unlocking the secrets that bind the two realms. Embrace your destiny, for the cosmic dance awaits your guidance."

With those cryptic words, the figure dissolved into the night, leaving Aadi standing alone along the Ghats. The air hummed with the residual energy of the encounter, and the artifact pulsed with a newfound intensity. Aadi left with a sense of purpose and a cascade of unanswered questions, pondered the significance of his role in the unfolding cosmic drama.

The encounter at the Ghats had marked a turning point, and Varanasi itself seemed to echo the figure's words through the ancient stones. Aadi, now both seeker and guardian, gazed upon the artifact with a newfound understanding. The river flowed with whispers, and the stars above held the promise of secrets waiting to be unveiled.

As the night embraced Varanasi in its cosmic embrace, Aadi set forth on a path that transcended the boundaries of the ordinary. The mysterious figure had ignited a spark within him, and the artifact became not just a relic but a beacon guiding him through the astral realms. The Ghats, witness to the encounter, awaited the next chapter in the unfolding saga of "The Astral Chronicles."

# Chapter 6: Visionary Whispers

**Aadi's visions become more frequent and vivid.**
**He begins to research ancient Indian mysticism.**

In the wake of the enigmatic encounter at the Ghats, Aditya "Aadi" Sharma found himself caught in a current of ethereal energy that surged through the ancient city of Varanasi. The artifact, now resonating with a cosmic frequency, had become a conduit for Aadi's burgeoning connection to the astral realms. The nights unfolded like a tapestry of visions, each more vivid and revealing than the last.

As Aadi slept, the astral plane welcomed him with open arms. Celestial landscapes stretched infinitely, and ethereal beings danced in patterns that mirrored the constellations. Aadi, once an observer, now found himself an active participant in the astral ballet, guided by unseen forces that whispered secrets of the universe.

These visionary whispers became a nightly ritual, an astral sojourn that transcended the confines of mortal understanding. Aadi's dreams became a sanctuary where ancient deities unfolded the mysteries of the cosmos. The symbols on the artifact took on a life of their own, weaving tales of forgotten epochs and celestial alignments that echoed through the astral tapestry.

The visions did not cease with the dawning sun; they lingered, leaving an imprint upon Aadi's waking consciousness. The boundaries between dream and reality blurred, and Varanasi itself seemed to shimmer with the residual energy of the astral dance. Aadi, compelled by a cosmic force, embarked on a quest to unravel the significance of the visions that whispered through the night.

In the heart of Varanasi, Aadi delved into the ancient texts and scriptures that spoke of mysticism woven into the city's very foundations. The Ghats, the temples, the winding alleys—all held fragments of esoteric knowledge waiting to be deciphered. Aadi, armed with the artifact and fueled by a thirst for understanding, immersed himself in the rich tapestry of ancient Indian mysticism.

He pored over manuscripts that spoke of celestial gateways and the language of the stars. The cosmic dance, described in cryptic verses, seemed to mirror the very visions that unfolded in Aadi's dreams. Varanasi, once a city of stone and history, now became a living library where the whispers of the ancients echoed through time.

As Aadi's research deepened, so did his connection to the artifact. The symbols, once enigmatic, began to reveal their secrets. Each stroke and curve held a resonance with the astral plane, as if the artifact itself was a conduit for the ancient knowledge that Varanasi guarded so closely.

The city, aware of Aadi's quest, responded with subtle shifts in energy. Pilgrims and priests spoke of a seeker who walked the fine line between worlds. Aadi's name became synonymous with the mystical forces that stirred within Varanasi, and the artifact, now recognized as a vessel of cosmic power, drew curious eyes and awed whispers.

Aadi, fueled by the visions and guided by the whispers of the astral, stood at the threshold of an ancient knowledge that held the key to the cosmic dance he was destined to lead. Varanasi, with its ancient stones and celestial energies, became both a teacher and a companion in Aadi's journey—a journey that would unfold in the pages of "The Astral Chronicles."

# Chapter 7: Unveiling the Mysteries

**Aadi deciphers a portion of the artifact's symbols.**
**Begins to suspect a connection to celestial realms.**

Varanasi, with its ancient soul and mystical aura, became the crucible where Aditya "Aadi" Sharma sought to unravel the enigma that lay within the artifact's symbols. Guided by the whispers of the astral and armed with an insatiable curiosity, Aadi immersed himself in the study of ancient Indian mysticism, threading through the labyrinthine alleys and the timeless Ghats that echoed with the wisdom of the ages.

Night after night, Aadi returned to the astral plane, where celestial beings beckoned with cryptic messages. In the waking world, he pored over manuscripts and scriptures, tracing the echoes of the astral dance in the ancient texts that Varanasi held in its embrace. As the city slept, Aadi's mind danced on the precipice of discovery, fueled by the cosmic energy that pulsed through the artifact.

It was during one such night, as the moon cast its silvery glow upon the Ghats, that Aadi's quest took a significant turn. With the artifact cradled in his hands, he delved into the symbols etched upon its surface, his fingers tracing the intricate patterns with newfound insight. The visions of the astral plane seemed to converge in that moment, guiding Aadi's deciphering of the enigmatic script.

As the symbols unfolded, a portion of the cosmic language revealed itself to Aadi's searching eyes. Celestial constellations, ancient mantras, and the rhythmic dance of stars—all encoded within the artifact's markings. Aadi, entranced by the convergence of the astral whispers and the deciphered symbols, began to suspect a connection that transcended the earthly realm.

The symbols hinted at a celestial language, a code that echoed the very language of the stars. Aadi's research led him to scriptures that spoke of astral gateways, celestial realms, and the cosmic balance that held the universe in harmony. The artifact, he realized, was not merely a relic of the past but a key that could unlock gateways to the celestial realms—the very realms glimpsed in his astral visions.

As Aadi unveiled the mysteries encoded within the symbols, a profound realization dawned upon him. The artifact, infused with the energy of the astral plane, acted as a bridge—a cosmic link between the earthly and the celestial. Varanasi, with its ancient energies and the artifact's newfound revelations, became a nexus where mortal and astral realms converged.

The city responded to Aadi's revelations with a subtle shift in energy. Pilgrims and residents, attuned to the mystical currents that flowed through Varanasi, sensed a cosmic dance taking shape. Aadi, now both an archaeologist and celestial seeker, stood at the crossroads of worlds, his understanding of the artifact propelling him into uncharted territories of the cosmic tapestry.

The symbols, once a cryptic language etched upon the artifact, now became a guide to celestial gateways and astral realms waiting to be explored. Aadi's suspicion of a connection to the celestial realms grew into a certainty—a certainty that would propel him further into the cosmic drama unfolding in the heart of Varanasi.

As the city slept under the watchful eyes of ancient deities, Aadi, armed with newfound knowledge and the artifact's cosmic resonance, stood ready to embark on a journey that transcended the limits of mortal understanding. The mysteries unveiled in Varanasi were not confined to its ancient stones but reached into the very fabric of the stars—a revelation that would echo through the chapters of "The Astral Chronicles."

# Chapter 8: An Unexpected Alliance

**Aadi crosses paths with Priya Mehta, an astrophysicist interested in celestial anomalies.**
**They join forces to investigate the artifact's origins.**

The cosmic energies of Varanasi, stirred by Aditya "Aadi" Sharma's revelations, set the stage for an unexpected convergence. As Aadi delved deeper into the mysteries encoded within the artifact, a force beyond the astral seemed to guide his steps. It was during one of his nocturnal explorations along the Ghats that destiny wove an unexpected alliance.

Under the expansive canvas of the night sky, adorned with stars that mirrored the symbols on the artifact, Aadi caught sight of a figure that seemed to materialize from the celestial tapestry. Priya Mehta, a brilliant astrophysicist with a keen interest in celestial anomalies, stood gazing at the stars with an intensity that mirrored Aadi's own curiosity.

Their eyes met, and recognition sparked—an acknowledgment of kindred spirits drawn together by the cosmic dance. Priya, her eyes reflecting the galaxies she studied, approached Aadi with a question that mirrored the enigma he sought to unravel. "Aditya Sharma, the archaeologist known for translating the inestimable content, right?" she inquired, her voice carrying the resonance of shared curiosity.

Aadi, intrigued by the unexpected encounter, nodded. The artifact, cradled in his hands, seemed to resonate in acknowledgment as if recognizing the convergence of two seekers destined to unravel the cosmic mysteries. Priya, with her background in astrophysics, sensed the celestial energy that pulsed through Aadi and the artifact.

As they exchanged stories of their individual quests, a realization dawned upon them—the convergence of their expertise held the key to a deeper understanding of the artifact's origins. The symbols on the relic, now deciphered to a significant extent by Aadi, echoed the patterns Priya observed in the celestial phenomena she studied.

Their alliance became more than a partnership; it became a cosmic symphony—a fusion of earthly archaeology and celestial science. Aadi's visions of the astral and Priya's knowledge of the stars intertwined, creating a synergy that transcended the boundaries of conventional understanding.

Together, Aadi and Priya embarked on a journey to trace the origins of the artifact. Varanasi, with its mystical energies and ancient echoes, became the starting point of their exploration. The Ghats, the temples, and the hidden corners of the city became a canvas where the alliance between archaeology and astrophysics painted a narrative that spanned both earthly and celestial realms.

As the duo delved into their investigation, the artifact responded to their shared quest. Its energy once confined to the hands of a lone archaeologist, now pulsed with an intensified rhythm—a cosmic heartbeat that echoed the union of Aadi and Priya's expertise.

The nights in Varanasi became a laboratory where celestial anomalies and ancient mysteries converged. Aadi's visions, now guided by Priya's scientific insights, gained clarity. The artifact, resonating with the energy of their alliance, became a beacon that illuminated the path to an ancient cosmic truth waiting to be unveiled.

An unexpected alliance forged under the cosmic gaze of Varanasi set the stage for a journey that would redefine the boundaries of earthly and celestial knowledge. Aadi and Priya, united by a common purpose, stood on the precipice of discovery, ready to unravel the cosmic threads woven into the fabric of "The Astral Chronicles."

# Chapter 9: Celestial Convergence

**Priya shares her research on celestial events matching Aadi's visions.**
**The duo plans an expedition to Hampi for further investigation.**

The alliance between Aditya "Aadi" Sharma and Priya Mehta deepened, like the intertwining orbits of celestial bodies destined to converge. In the heart of Varanasi, where ancient energies whispered through the labyrinthine alleys, Aadi

and Priya continued their quest to unravel the cosmic mysteries encoded within the artifact.

Under the expansive night sky, Priya shared her meticulous research on celestial events. As Aadi recounted his visions of the astral, Priya's eyes widened with recognition. The patterns in the stars mirrored the symbols on the artifact, creating a cosmic tapestry that spanned the realms of both earthly and celestial wonders.

"The celestial events you've described," Priya began, her voice carrying the resonance of revelation, "aligns perfectly with my observations. It's as if the stars themselves are echoing the astral dance you've experienced. The artifact, Aadi, is not just a relic—it's a celestial map, a guide to cosmic events waiting to unfold."

Aadi, his heart resonating with the cosmic harmony of their discoveries, nodded in agreement. The alliance between archaeology and astrophysics became a fusion of earthly wisdom and celestial insight. Varanasi, with its ancient stones and mystical echoes, bore witness to the convergence of their knowledge.

As the duo delved into the correlation between Aadi's visions and celestial phenomena, a realization dawned upon them—the next phase of their journey would take them beyond Varanasi. The artifact, pulsing with energy, seemed to beckon them toward Hampi, the forgotten empire where the ruins concealed secrets waiting to be unveiled.

In the heart of Varanasi, Aadi and Priya planned their expedition to Hampi—a pilgrimage of discovery that would transcend the boundaries of both earthly and celestial realms. The artifacts' symbols, decoded by Aadi, held the promise of celestial convergence that awaited them amidst the ancient ruins.

Their alliance became a beacon, drawing upon the energies of the cosmos to guide their path. Priya's scientific precision and Aadi's intuitive connection to the astral merged into a synergy that defied conventional understanding. The artifact, now recognized as a cosmic key, resonated with the celestial map Priya had deciphered.

As they prepared for the expedition, the city of Varanasi seemed to bless their journey. The river whispered ancient hymns, and the stars above sparkled with anticipation. Pilgrims and priests, sensing the cosmic dance unfolding in their midst, offered silent prayers for the seekers whose quest transcended mortal boundaries.

Under the celestial canopy, Aadi and Priya set forth on a journey to Hampi. The artifact, cradled in Aadi's hands, seemed to vibrate with anticipation. The cosmic convergence they sought, a tapestry woven with stars and astral echoes, awaited them amidst the ancient stones of Hampi.

Varanasi, with its mystical energies and the echoes of their alliance, watched as the seekers embarked on a pilgrimage that would unveil the celestial truths encoded within the artifact. The next chapter of "The Astral Chronicles" beckoned, promising a celestial convergence that would reshape the destinies of mortal and astral realms alike.

# Chapter 10: Departure to Hampi

**Aadi and Priya embark on a journey to Hampi accompanied by Rajveer Kapoor.**
**The trio's dynamics begin to take shape.**

Under the watchful gaze of Varanasi's ancient deities, Aditya "Aadi" Sharma and Priya Mehta prepared to embark on a journey to Hampi—a quest that promised to unravel the celestial mysteries encoded within the artifact. The cosmic convergence they sought waited amidst the ruins of the forgotten empire, where ancient stones held the echoes of an age long past.

As Aadi and Priya readied themselves for the expedition, a third figure emerged—a man with a presence as enigmatic as the celestial dance they sought to understand. Rajveer Kapoor, a historian with a penchant for untold stories, joined the alliance. His eyes, like the artifacts' symbols, held a glint of recognition, as if he, too, had glimpsed the cosmic truths waiting to be unveiled.

The trio's dynamics began to take shape—a fusion of Aadi's intuitive connection to the astral, Priya's scientific precision, and Rajveer's historical insights. Varanasi, with its ancient energies, bestowed its blessings upon the seekers as they set forth on a journey that spanned the boundaries of both time and space.

The expedition to Hampi became a pilgrimage of discovery—a celestial odyssey guided by the resonance of the artifact. Aadi, Priya, and Rajveer navigated the winding roads that led from Varanasi's mystic embrace to the silent echoes of Hampi's ancient stones. The artifact, cradled in Aadi's hands, seemed to vibrate with an energy that mirrored the trio's shared purpose.

As they journeyed, the dynamics between the three seekers unfolded. Aadi, the visionary with a connection to the astral, found resonance in Priya's meticulous research. Her scientific insights grounded his intuitive understanding, creating a synergy that bridged the earthly and celestial realms. Rajveer, with his historical acumen, wove the narrative of Hampi's forgotten empire into their cosmic exploration.

The road to Hampi became a stage where their individual strengths intertwined. Aadi's visions, Priya's celestial insights, and Rajveer's historical context merged into a narrative that transcended the limits of their individual expertise. The artifact, pulsing with the energy of their collective purpose, seemed to guide their steps toward the heart of the ancient ruins.

As they reached Hampi, the city of stones whispered secrets that transcended the ages. The ruins, bathed in the golden glow of the setting sun, held the promise of a celestial convergence that echoed through the corridors of time. The artifact's symbols, now familiar to the trio, seemed to respond to the energies of Hampi's silent echoes.

The trio, standing amidst the ancient stones, felt the weight of destiny upon their shoulders. The artifact, cradled in Aadi's hands, resonated with the celestial map Priya had deciphered and the historical tales Rajveer had unveiled. The cosmic convergence they sought waited in the heart of Hampi—a convergence that would reshape the destinies of mortal and astral realms alike.

As the sun dipped below the horizon, casting shadows upon the ruins, Aadi, Priya, and Rajveer stood united by a purpose that transcended the boundaries of individual quests. The next chapter of "The Astral Chronicles" unfolded in the ancient city of Hampi, where the seekers stood on the threshold of celestial truths waiting to be unveiled.

# Chapter 11: The Forgotten Empire

**Introduction to Hampi's rich history and mystical aura.**
**The team explores ancient ruins, searching for clues.**

Hampi, the forgotten empire, lay nestled amidst the boulders and palm groves, its silent ruins echoing the whispers of an age long past. As Aditya "Aadi" Sharma, Priya Mehta, and Rajveer Kapoor stepped into the heart of the ancient city, they were enveloped by Hampi's rich history and mystical aura.

The city, once a bustling capital of the Vijayanagara Empire, now stood in silent testimony to the passage of centuries. Crumbling temples and majestic ruins adorned the landscape, each stone holding fragments of untold stories waiting to be unraveled. Hampi, with its intricate carvings and silent echoes, became the canvas upon which the seekers would paint the next chapter of their cosmic journey.

Rajveer, the historian, shared tales of Hampi's glorious past—a time when the Vijayanagara Empire flourished, creating a cultural and architectural marvel that captivated the known world. Temples adorned with intricate carvings, grand palaces, and bustling marketplaces once filled the city with life. The remnants of that opulence now lay scattered across the landscape, embraced by the encroaching embrace of nature.

As the team explored the ancient ruins, the artifact pulsated with rhythmic energy, responding to the celestial map Priya had deciphered. The symbols on the artifact seemed to resonate with the carvings that adorned the temples—patterns that mirrored the constellations in the night sky. Aadi's visions, once confined to Varanasi, expanded into the celestial tapestry woven into Hampi's stones.

The Virupaksha Temple, dedicated to Lord Shiva, stood as a sentinel at the heart of Hampi. Its towering Gopuram reached for the heavens, adorned with intricate sculptures that told tales of celestial beings and cosmic events. Aadi, Priya, and Rajveer traced the carvings, seeking clues that could unlock the celestial mysteries hidden within the city's silent corridors.

As the team delved deeper into the ruins, they discovered hidden chambers and secret passages that spoke of a connection between the earthly and celestial realms. Aadi's visions became more vivid, guided by the astral energy that resonated with Hampi's stones. Priya, her scientific gaze keen, documented the alignments of celestial events with the ancient architecture.

In the tranquil moments between exploration and discovery, the team sensed the subtle shifts in energy—the cosmic convergence they sought drawing near. The artifact, now recognized as a cosmic key, responded to the celestial resonance embedded within Hampi's very foundation.

The night in Hampi was a symphony of stars, and the team gathered at the Tungabhadra River, where the celestial reflections mirrored the mysteries unfolding in the ancient city. Aadi, Priya, and Rajveer, united by purpose and destiny, stood at the crossroads of mortal and astral realms.

As the night embraced Hampi in its cosmic aura, the seekers prepared for the next phase of their exploration. The forgotten empire, with its silent stones and celestial echoes, held the key to the cosmic dance encoded within the artifact. The next chapter of "The Astral Chronicles" waited, as the seekers stood on the threshold of celestial truths that transcended time and space.

# Chapter 12: Astral Echoes

**Aadi experiences astral echoes within Hampi's ruins.**
**The trio encounters the first signs of celestial convergence.**

The night in Hampi was alive with the cosmic energies that lingered within the ancient ruins. Aditya "Aadi" Sharma, Priya Mehta, and Rajveer Kapoor standing amidst the silent stones, felt the celestial vibrations that echoed through the corridors of time. As the moon cast its silvery glow upon Hampi's forgotten empire, Aadi's connection to the astral deepened, and the ruins responded with astral echoes.

In the heart of the Virupaksha Temple, Aadi closed his eyes, allowing the resonance of the artifact to guide him. The ancient carvings seemed to come to life, and the stones whispered secrets that transcended the earthly realm. Aadi's visions, once confined to dreams, now unfolded within the waking reality of Hampi, revealing glimpses of celestial beings and astral realms that intersected with the city's silent corridors.

Priya, her scientific gaze attuned to the celestial alignments, observed the subtle shifts in the atmosphere. The night sky above Hampi held a brilliance that mirrored the patterns on the artifact. Stars seemed to align with the carvings, creating a celestial dance that unfolded above and below.

Rajveer, the historian, traced the stories etched into the stones. Tales of gods and goddesses, celestial events, and the cosmic balance that once governed the Vijayanagara Empire emerged from the intricate carvings. The forgotten empire, it seemed, held a deeper connection to the astral realms than history had recorded.

As Aadi moved through the ruins, the astral echoes intensified. Celestial beings, their forms luminous and ethereal, danced across the cosmic tapestry woven into Hampi's stones. The artifact in Aadi's hands pulsed with otherworldly energy, responding to the astral resonance that unfolded within the ancient city.

The trio, united by purpose, ventured into Hampi's lesser-explored corners. Hidden chambers and secret passages revealed themselves, each bearing the mark of the celestial dance. Aadi's visions, guided by the astral echoes, led the team to an ancient observatory—an intricate structure that once served as a gateway between the earthly and celestial realms.

As they stood within the observatory, the night sky above Hampi became a canvas painted with celestial hues. Stars aligned in patterns that mirrored the symbols on the artifact, creating a celestial convergence that transcended the ordinary. Aadi, Priya, and Rajveer witnessed the first signs of the cosmic dance—the intertwining of mortal and astral realms.

The artifact, now infused with the energy of Hampi's astral echoes, seemed to radiate with a newfound intensity. Aadi, his senses attuned to the celestial vibrations, felt a profound connection to the ancient city. The ruins, once silent witnesses to centuries gone by, resonated with the seekers' quest for celestial truths.

Under the cosmic canopy of Hampi, Aadi, Priya, and Rajveer stood on the precipice of a revelation. The astral echoes within the ruins whispered of a celestial convergence that awaited them—a convergence that would reshape the destinies of mortal and astral realms alike.

As the night deepened, Hampi's stones held the promise of a cosmic dance that transcended the boundaries of time and space. The artifact, now a beacon of celestial energy, pulsed with anticipation, marking the beginning of a celestial journey that would echo through the ages in "The Astral Chronicles."

# Chapter 13: Trials of Hampi

**The team faces challenges and puzzles in the ruins.**
**Aadi's mystical powers are put to the test.**

In the heart of Hampi's forgotten empire, where celestial echoes lingered and the cosmic dance unfolded, Aditya "Aadi" Sharma, Priya Mehta, and Rajveer Kapoor faced a series of trials that tested the limits of mortal and astral realms alike. The ancient ruins, now a labyrinth of celestial mysteries, presented challenges that demanded both earthly wisdom and astral insight.

The team navigated the hidden chambers and secret passages that led deeper into Hampi's silent embrace. Carvings on the walls depicted trials faced by ancient seekers, each puzzle a testament to the connection between the earthly and celestial planes. Aadi, with his mystical powers attuned to the astral, sensed the energy of the trials that awaited them.

The first trial unfolded within the ruins of the Lotus Mahal, an ornate structure that once stood as a testament to Vijayanagara's architectural prowess. As the team entered the regal halls, celestial symbols adorned the walls, intertwining with intricate patterns that seemed to shift with each step. Priya, with her scientific acumen, deciphered the alignments that mirrored the stars above.

The trial challenged the team to unlock the celestial gateways hidden within the Lotus Mahal. Aadi, guided by the astral echoes, traced the symbols on the artifact, seeking resonance with the celestial patterns. Priya's meticulous observations and Rajveer's historical insights became essential threads in the cosmic tapestry they wove.

As the team deciphered the celestial puzzle, the Lotus Mahal responded with a subtle shift in energy. The walls seemed to breathe, and the air hummed with the astral resonance. The artifact, now a key infused with celestial energy, opened gateways that transcended the earthly boundaries.

The second trial led the team to the Hampi Bazaar, where marketplaces once bustled with life. The carvings on the pillars depicted a celestial market where gods and celestial beings exchanged cosmic energies. Aadi, his mystical powers growing with each trial, felt a connection to the astral market that echoed through the ages.

The trial demanded an understanding of celestial commerce—a dance of energies that required Aadi to navigate the astral bazaar. Priya and Rajveer, attuned to the cosmic patterns, provided insights that guided Aadi through the celestial marketplace. The artifact, resonating with the trials, pulsed with a rhythmic beat.

As Aadi moved through the astral bazaar, encountering celestial beings and mystical energies, the team witnessed the convergence of earthly and celestial commerce. The Hampi Bazaar, now a cosmic crossroads, responded to the seekers' understanding of the astral dance. The artifact, now a cosmic compass, pointed toward the next trial awaiting them.

The third trial unfolded in the ancient ruins of the Elephant Stables. Celestial carvings depicted elephants adorned with celestial symbols, their majestic forms embodying the cosmic balance. Aadi's mystical powers, honed by the trials, were put to the test as the team faced challenges that blurred the lines between the earthly and astral planes.

The trial demanded a communion with the astral elephants—a dance that required Aadi to channel the celestial energies embodied within the majestic creatures. Priya and Rajveer, their insights into the celestial balance deepening, supported Aadi in his mystical endeavor.

The artifact, now a conduit for astral energies, resonated with the heartbeat of the celestial elephants.

As Aadi communed with the astral beings, the Elephant Stables seemed to vibrate with a celestial rhythm. The ancient ruins, now a sanctuary of cosmic energies, acknowledged the seekers' mastery of the astral trials. The artifact, now a symbol of celestial harmony, pulsed with an energy that transcended the earthly realm.

The trials of Hampi, a cosmic odyssey that tested the team's earthly and astral faculties, marked a turning point in their journey. The seekers, united by purpose and destiny, stood ready to face the next challenges that awaited them in the heart of the forgotten empire. The celestial dance, now in full motion, echoed through the ancient stones, guiding the seekers toward the revelations that lay beyond the trials of Hampi in "The Astral Chronicles."

# Chapter 14: The Veil Thins

**The group discovers an ancient chamber where the veil between realms is thin.**
**A glimpse of astral energies becomes more pronounced.**

Deep within the heart of Hampi's labyrinthine ruins, where celestial trials had tested the seekers' earthly and astral faculties, Aditya "Aadi" Sharma, Priya Mehta, and Rajveer Kapoor stumbled upon an ancient chamber. The air within this hidden sanctuary resonated with a mystical energy—a subtle hum that hinted at a convergence of realms. As the seekers entered the chamber, they discovered that the veil between mortal and astral realms was thinning.

Carvings adorned the chamber's walls, depicting cosmic gateways and astral beings passing between worlds. The symbols on the artifact, now infused with the energies of Hampi's celestial trials, pulsed in harmony with the astral currents that lingered in the air. Aadi, his mystical powers honed through the trials, sensed the thinning veil and the astral energies that waited beyond.

As the seekers delved deeper into the chamber, a celestial glow permeated the air. The stones seemed to shimmer with the residue of astral energies, creating an ethereal ambiance that transcended the ordinary. Aadi, Priya, and Rajveer, their senses attuned to the subtle shifts in cosmic currents, felt the veil between realms growing ever thinner.

In the center of the chamber, a cosmic portal revealed itself—a gateway that beckoned the seekers to glimpse the astral realms that lay beyond. The artifact, now a conduit for celestial energies, resonated with the portal's call. Aadi, guided by his connection to the astral, approached the gateway with a sense of anticipation.

As Aadi touched the artifact to the celestial portal, the veil between realms thinned further. A cascade of astral energies enveloped the seekers, transporting them to the threshold of the celestial dance. The chamber, now a nexus where mortal and astral energies intertwined, echoed with the whispers of celestial beings and the cosmic symphony that reverberated through the ages.

Priya and Rajveer, standing alongside Aadi, witnessed the astral energies taking tangible form. Celestial beings, their luminous forms dancing in patterns that mirrored the constellations, greeted the seekers. The artifact, now a beacon that bridged the realms, pulsed with an intensity that transcended the earthly confines.

The seekers, now on the cusp of the astral realms, experienced a profound connection to the cosmic dance. Aadi's visions once confined to dreams and fleeting glimpses, became a tangible reality within the celestial chamber. Priya, her scientific gaze widened by the astral revelations, documented the convergence of mortal and astral energies. Rajveer, the historian, witnessed the unfolding of a cosmic tale that transcended the pages of earthly history.

As the seekers lingered at the threshold of the celestial portal, the veil between realms continued to thin. The chamber, now a sanctum where mortal and astral energies intertwined, became a testament to the seekers' journey through Hampi's forgotten empire. The artifact, pulsating with celestial resonance, marked a turning point in their cosmic odyssey.

In the heart of Hampi's celestial chamber, the seekers stood as witnesses to the thinning veil between realms. The astral energies, once elusive and mysterious, now flowed around them, offering glimpses of a cosmic tapestry waiting to be unveiled. The next phase of their journey, now intricately woven with astral threads, beckoned the seekers deeper into the realms beyond—the unfolding chapters of "The Astral Chronicles."

# Chapter 15: Guardian of Secrets

**A guardian figure appears, testing the trio's worthiness.
Aadi's connection to the artifact deepens.**

In the heart of Hampi's celestial chamber, where the veil between realms thinned and the astral energies whispered cosmic secrets, a guardian figure materialized before Aditya "Aadi" Sharma, Priya Mehta, and Rajveer Kapoor. The guardian, an ethereal being adorned with celestial symbols that mirrored those on the artifact, stood as the arbiter of cosmic knowledge, testing the trio's worthiness to venture further into the astral realms.

The guardian's luminous form emanated a sense of ancient wisdom, and its eyes held the depth of eons. Aadi, attuned to the astral energies, felt a resonance with the celestial figure—a recognition that transcended words. The artifact, cradled in Aadi's hands, pulsed with an intensity that mirrored the guardian's presence.

As the celestial guardian surveyed the seekers, it gestured toward the artifact, a silent invitation for Aadi to unveil the cosmic truths encoded within. The symbols on the artifact, now intricately woven with the energies of Hampi's celestial trials, seemed to respond to the guardian's cosmic gaze.

The Guardian spoke not in words but in the language of astral resonance. Aadi, Priya, and Rajveer, united by purpose and destiny, felt the weight of the guardian's scrutiny—a test that reached beyond the earthly boundaries and delved into the depths of their connection to the astral realms.

Aadi, guided by the cosmic intuition that had shaped his journey, allowed the artifact to channel the celestial energies within. As he touched the symbols on its surface, a surge of astral power emanated from the artifact, creating a luminous aura that enveloped the celestial chamber. The Guardian, its gaze unyielding, witnessed the seekers' communion with the cosmic forces.

Priya, her scientific gaze now tempered by the mystical insights gained in Hampi, observed the interplay between the artifact's symbols and the celestial guardian. Rajveer, the historian, recognized the echoes of celestial tales woven into the guardian's form—a living testament to the cosmic balance that governed the astral realms.

The guardian, satisfied with the seekers' attunement to the celestial energies, bestowed upon them a cosmic blessing. Aadi, as the chosen guardian of the artifact, felt a profound connection deepening within him. The celestial symbols, once enigmatic, now seemed to flow through his veins, intertwining with his very essence.

As the guardian faded into the astral currents, the seekers were left standing in the luminous aftermath of the cosmic encounter. Aadi, Priya, and Rajveer, now marked by the celestial blessing, sensed a heightened connection to the astral realms. The artifact, now a conduit for celestial energies, hummed with a resonance that echoed through the ancient stones of Hampi.

The celestial chamber, once a nexus of cosmic trials, became a sanctum where the seekers' worthiness was acknowledged by the guardian of secrets. The thinning veil between realms, now marked by the seekers' attunement to the astral energies, beckoned them further into the unfolding chapters of "The Astral Chronicles." Aadi's connection to the artifact, now fused with celestial power, marked a pivotal moment in their cosmic odyssey—a moment that would shape the destinies of mortal and astral realms alike.

# Chapter 16: Revelations in the Stars

**Priya deciphers celestial patterns linking the artifact to astral gateways.**
**The team realizes the artifact's role in astral travel.**

Emboldened by the celestial blessing bestowed upon them in Hampi's cosmic chamber, Aditya "Aadi" Sharma, Priya Mehta, and Rajveer Kapoor gathered beneath the night sky, where stars adorned the canvas like celestial jewels. The artifact, now resonant with the guardian's blessing, seemed to hum with eager anticipation. As the seekers stood on the sacred ground of Hampi, Priya, the astrophysicist with a keen eye for celestial patterns, unraveled revelations that bridged the earthly and astral realms.

Priya, her gaze fixed upon the stars, deciphered celestial patterns that mirrored the symbols on the artifact. The constellations above Hampi, once distant and unreachable, seemed to align with the astral gateways hinted at by the guardian. The artifact, pulsating with celestial energies, responded to Priya's insights, creating a cosmic dialogue that transcended earthly understanding.

The team gathered around Priya as she unveiled the celestial revelations. "The symbols on the artifact," she began, her voice carrying the resonance of astral insight, "are not just representations; they are cosmic coordinates, linking us to astral gateways scattered across the celestial tapestry."

As Priya spoke, the stars above Hampi seemed to rearrange themselves, forming patterns that echoed the symbols on the artifact. Aadi, his connection to the astral deepening, felt the cosmic currents responding to Priya's revelations. The artifact, now recognized as a key to celestial gateways, pulsed with an energy that echoed the stars' alignment.

Rajveer, the historian, recognized the echoes of ancient myths in Priya's words. "These passages," he considered, "have been talked about in the stories of divine beings and heavenly creatures. They connect realms beyond mortal understanding—a bridge between the earthly and astral planes."

The realization dawned upon the seekers—the artifact held the key to astral travel. The symbols, once cryptic, now became a celestial map guiding the way through the cosmic currents. Priya, with her astrophysical insights, traced the connections between earthly and celestial energies, unraveling the mysteries encoded within the artifact.

As the team embraced the cosmic revelations, Aadi touched the artifact, allowing its energy to resonate with the celestial coordinates. The night sky responded, creating a celestial dance that mirrored the astral gateways awaiting discovery. The artifact, now a beacon infused with celestial power, seemed to transcend the boundaries of time and space.

Under the celestial canopy of Hampi, the seekers realized their role as cosmic travelers. The ancient stones, the guardian's blessing, and Priya's celestial revelations converged to unveil the artifact's purpose—to serve as a key to the astral gateways that connected realms beyond mortal comprehension.

With newfound clarity, the team prepared for the next phase of their journey. The artifact, cradled in Aadi's hands, held the promise of astral travel—a cosmic odyssey that would take them beyond the earthly confines. The stars above Hampi, now aligned with the seekers' purpose, guided the way to astral gateways that awaited exploration.

The revelations in the stars marked a turning point in "The Astral Chronicles." Aadi, Priya, and Rajveer, bound by destiny and purpose, stood on the threshold of celestial truths, ready to embark on a journey that would transcend the boundaries of mortal and astral realms alike.

# Chapter 17: Night Sky Dance

**The trio experiences a celestial event that amplifies their powers. Aadi gains control over astral projections.**

As the seekers stood beneath the celestial canopy of Hampi, where the stars seemed to shimmer with newfound purpose, a cosmic event unfolded—a night sky dance that would amplify their earthly and astral powers. The artifact, now recognized as a key to astral gateways, pulsed with an energy that resonated with the celestial patterns above.

The night sky, adorned with constellations that mirrored the symbols on the artifact, began to shift. Celestial energies descended like shimmering curtains, enveloping Aditya "Aadi" Sharma, Priya Mehta, and Rajveer Kapoor in a luminous embrace. The air hummed with astral currents, and the ancient stones of Hampi seemed to vibrate in response to the cosmic dance.

Aadi, with the artifact cradled in his hands, felt the surge of astral energy coursing through his veins. The celestial event, a convergence of earthly and astral forces, awakened a latent power within the seekers. Priya, her astrophysical senses heightened by the celestial dance, observed the stars aligning in patterns that echoed the astral gateways encoded within the artifact.

Rajveer, the historian, recognized the echoes of celestial myths manifesting in the night sky. "This is more than just a dance of stars," he exclaimed. "It's a cosmic symphony, and we are the players in a celestial orchestra."

As the celestial dance reached its zenith, Aadi felt a surge of power within him. The artifact, now a conduit for the amplified astral energies, responded to Aadi's connection to the astral realms. In a moment of profound realization, Aadi extended his consciousness beyond the confines of his physical form.

Astral projections, guided by Aadi's newfound control, unfolded like ethereal wings. He hovered above the ancient stones of Hampi, his form luminous and transcendent. The night sky, now a canvas for astral energies, echoed with the whispers of celestial beings and the cosmic currents that flowed through the seekers.

Priya and Rajveer, witnessing Aadi's astral projection, felt the resonance of his newfound abilities. The artifact, now infused with amplified astral energies, hummed in harmony with the celestial dance. The trio, united by destiny and purpose, stood at the nexus of mortal and astral realms, their powers magnified by the cosmic event.

As Aadi explored the astral plane, the celestial dance intensified. The stars above Hampi responded to his astral presence, creating patterns that echoed the symbols on the artifact. Priya, with her astrophysical insights, and Rajveer, with his historical perspective, marveled at the cosmic revelations unfolding before them.

In the midst of the celestial dance, the seekers realized the extent of their powers. Aadi, now a master of astral projections, guided the team through the astral gateways hinted at by the guardian. The artifact, pulsating with amplified energies, became a beacon that bridged the realms beyond mortal understanding.

The night sky dance marked a transformative moment in "The Astral Chronicles." Aadi, Priya, and Rajveer, now attuned to the amplified astral energies, stood ready to navigate the celestial gateways that awaited exploration. The ancient stones of Hampi, witnesses to the cosmic symphony, seemed to echo with the celestial tales that transcended time and space. The next chapter of their journey beckoned—an odyssey through the astral realms guided by the powers awakened in the night sky dance.

# Chapter 18: Rishikesh Calling

**The group decides to journey to Rishikesh for spiritual training.**
**A sense of urgency as astral imbalances becomes more apparent.**

Amidst the lingering echoes of the celestial dance in Hampi, Aditya "Aadi" Sharma, Priya Mehta, and Rajveer Kapoor gathered to deliberate their next steps. The amplified astral energies channeled through the artifact, urged the seekers toward a new destination—an ancient city renowned for its spiritual aura and mystic teachings. Rishikesh, nestled in the foothills of the Himalayas, called to the trio as they felt the urgency of astral imbalances growing more apparent.

The artifact, now pulsating with celestial power, seemed to resonate with the energy of Rishikesh—the sacred city where the Ganges flowed in a divine dance, and the Himalayan peaks whispered the secrets of the cosmos. Priya, with her astrophysical insights, sensed a convergence of celestial energies in the spiritual haven. Rajveer, the historian, recognized the threads of ancient wisdom woven into Rishikesh's mystical tapestry.

"The astral imbalances are becoming more pronounced," Priya observed. "Rishikesh, with its spiritual sanctuaries and ancient teachings, might hold the key to restoring harmony to the astral realms."

Rajveer nodded in agreement, his historical perspective resonating with the urgency in Priya's words. "The ancients sought Rishikesh for spiritual enlightenment and cosmic balance. Perhaps our journey there will uncover the truths hidden within the astral imbalances."

Aadi, his connection to the astral realms deepened by the night sky dance, felt a sense of destiny unfolding. The artifact, now a beacon of celestial power, guided the seekers toward the spiritual haven that awaited their arrival. The urgency of astral imbalances propelled them toward Rishikesh, where the Ganges' sacred waters whispered of ancient truths.

The decision was made—a journey to Rishikesh for spiritual training and cosmic insights. The seekers, bound by purpose and destiny, set forth on a path that transcended the ordinary. The artifact, cradled in Aadi's hands, pulsed with an intensity that mirrored the urgency of the astral imbalances.

As the seekers embarked on the road to Rishikesh, a sense of anticipation hung in the air. The Ganges, with its sacred currents, seemed to beckon them toward the cosmic truths waiting to be unveiled. The Himalayan peaks, veiled in mist and ancient wisdom, watched over the seekers' journey as if acknowledging the significance of their quest.

Rishikesh called to the seekers—a city where mystics sought communion with the divine, and the astral imbalances could find equilibrium. The artifact, now a key to the astral gateways, held the promise of insights that would shape the destinies of mortal and astral realms alike.

As the seekers ventured toward Rishikesh, the urgency of their quest echoed in the rustling leaves and the sacred chants that carried on the breeze. The next chapter of "The Astral Chronicles" unfolded on the road to spiritual enlightenment—a journey through the Himalayan mystique guided by the celestial energies that pulsed within the artifact.

# Chapter 19: The Mystic Trainers

**Introduction to mystical mentors in Rishikesh.**
**The trio begins their spiritual training.**

In the heart of Rishikesh, where the Ganges flowed with the grace of ancient wisdom and the Himalayan peaks embraced the sky in silent majesty, Aditya "Aadi" Sharma, Priya Mehta, and Rajveer Kapoor arrived at the threshold of spiritual enlightenment. The urgency of astral imbalances lingered in the air, guiding them to the sacred city's mystical sanctuaries, where the ancient arts of cosmic balance were taught by mystic trainers who held the keys to celestial insights.

The seekers, bearing the artifact pulsating with celestial power, were welcomed into the realm of the mystic trainers. The mentors, with eyes that held the depth of cosmic mysteries, recognized the seekers' purpose and destiny. Each mentor embodied the ancient teachings of Rishikesh—knowledge that transcended the earthly and astral realms.

The first mentor, a sage with a flowing beard and eyes that sparkled with starlight, introduced himself as Guru Amara. His teachings delved into the cosmic dance of energies—the interplay between earthly and astral forces that shaped the fabric of existence. Aadi, Priya, and Rajveer listened with rapt attention as Guru Amara unveiled the secrets encoded within the celestial symbols on the artifact.

Under Guru Amara's guidance, the seekers began their spiritual training. Aadi, attuned to the astral energies, learned to navigate the celestial gateways with greater precision. Priya, with her astrophysical insights, deepened her understanding of the celestial patterns that guided the artifact's power. Rajveer, the historian, uncovered the ancient myths and tales that echoed in the teachings of Rishikesh.

The second mentor, a yogi whose body seemed to flow with the currents of the Ganges, introduced herself as Yogini Surya. Her teachings focused on the balance of mind, body, and spirit—a harmony that resonated with the seekers' quest for astral equilibrium. The trio, guided by Yogini Surya, practiced ancient yogic techniques that strengthened their connection to the celestial energies.

As the seekers delved into their spiritual training, the urgency of astral imbalances became more apparent. The mystic trainers, with their cosmic insight, sensed the unfolding cosmic dance that demanded the seekers' mastery. The artifact, now a conduit for celestial energies, responded to the seekers' growing proficiency, pulsing with a rhythmic beat that echoed the mystic trainers' guidance.

The third mentor, a seer with eyes that mirrored the reflection of the Ganges' sacred waters, introduced himself as Rishi Varun. His teachings centered on the ancient art of astral projection—a skill that would empower the seekers to traverse the astral realms with purpose and clarity. Aadi, under Rishi Varun's guidance, honed his ability to control astral projections, navigating the celestial currents with newfound mastery.

As the seekers progressed through their spiritual training, the mystic trainers unveiled the deeper mysteries of Rishikesh. The Ganges, with its purifying waters, became a conduit for astral energies. The Himalayan peaks, veiled in mist and ancient wisdom, whispered tales of cosmic journeys that transcended mortal understanding.

The seekers, now adept in the arts of cosmic balance, stood at the intersection of ancient wisdom and celestial insights. The artifact, resonant with the teachings of Rishikesh, held the promise of astral equilibrium—a harmony that would restore balance to the imbalances unfolding in the cosmic dance.

In the sacred spaces of Rishikesh, under the guidance of the mystic trainers, Aadi, Priya, and Rajveer embraced their roles as cosmic seekers. The next chapter of "The Astral Chronicles" beckoned—a journey through the Himalayan mystique, guided by the celestial energies that pulsed within the artifact and the teachings of Rishikesh's wise mentors.

# Chapter 20: Inner Realms Unveiled

**Aadi confronts his inner shadows during meditation.**
**The team learns to navigate the astral plane consciously.**

In the serene landscapes of Rishikesh, where the Ganges whispered ancient hymns and the Himalayan peaks stood as silent guardians of cosmic knowledge, Aditya "Aadi" Sharma, Priya Mehta, and Rajveer Kapoor delved deeper into their spiritual training. Under the guidance of the mystic trainers, the seekers aimed to unveil the inner realms that mirrored the astral imbalances echoing in the cosmic dance.

One evening, as the sun dipped below the horizon and the celestial energies painted the sky with hues of cosmic resonance, Aadi embarked on a profound meditation. In the quiet sanctum of Rishikesh, he confronted the shadows that lurked within—the echoes of past fears and uncharted territories of the astral realms. The artifact, now a conduit for celestial energies, cradled in Aadi's hands, resonated with the depth of his meditation.

As Aadi delved into the recesses of his consciousness, the inner realms unveiled themselves. Shadows danced on the edges of his awareness, challenging him to confront the fears that bound him to the earthly plane. The mystic trainers, sensing Aadi's journey into the depths of his soul, stood as silent witnesses to the cosmic enfoldment.

In the astral plane of his inner realms, Aadi encountered echoes of his past—the moments of doubt, the shadows of unfulfilled potential, and the fears that held him captive. The celestial currents, guided by the artifact's resonance, responded to Aadi's determination to navigate the astral plane consciously.

Priya and Rajveer, under the guidance of Yogini Surya and Rishi Varun, respectively, embarked on their own journeys within. The celestial energies pulsed within them, amplifying their consciousness as they navigated the astral realms of their inner landscapes. The Ganges, with its sacred currents, became a river of cosmic wisdom that flowed through the seekers' meditative states.

As the seekers confronted their inner shadows, the mystic trainers infused the teachings of Rishikesh into their spiritual training. The Ganges, reflecting the stars above, became a celestial mirror that revealed the seekers' true essence. The Himalayan peaks, veiled in mist and ancient wisdom, whispered guidance that transcended the earthly plane.

Aadi, anchored by the artifact's celestial power, faced the shadows with unwavering resolve. The astral imbalances, once hidden in the depths of his consciousness, now surfaced as challenges to be overcome. The mystic trainers, with eyes that held the depth of cosmic insight, supported Aadi in his journey, recognizing the transformative power of conscious navigation through the astral realms.

In the cosmic dance of inner realms, the seekers emerged with newfound clarity. The shadows, once formidable, now bowed to the seekers' mastery of the astral plane. The artifact, resonating with the seekers' heightened consciousness, pulsed with a luminous energy that echoed the celestial insights gained in Rishikesh.

Aadi, Priya, and Rajveer, united by the shared journey through their inner landscapes, stood as beacons of cosmic wisdom. The mystic trainers, their teachings woven into the seekers' very beings, acknowledged the transformative power of conscious astral navigation. The next phase of their journey awaited—a journey that would see the seekers navigate the astral plane consciously, restoring balance to the cosmic dance and unveiling the truths hidden within the inner realms.

# Chapter 21: Bonds Strengthened

**Characters' relationships deepen during their time in Rishikesh.**
**A growing sense of purpose and unity.**

In the sacred embrace of Rishikesh, where the Ganges flowed with the purity of ancient wisdom and the Himalayan peaks stood as witnesses to cosmic revelations, the bonds between Aditya "Aadi" Sharma, Priya Mehta, and Rajveer Kapoor deepened. Under the guidance of the mystic trainers, the seekers' relationships flourished in the fertile grounds of spiritual enlightenment, forging a unity that transcended earthly ties.

As the seekers navigated the astral realms of their inner landscapes, the shared experiences wove a tapestry of understanding and camaraderie. Aadi, with his mastery over astral projections, guided Priya and Rajveer through the celestial currents. The artifact, pulsating with celestial power, became a beacon that illuminated the seekers' path in the spiritual haven of Rishikesh.

The mystic trainers, recognizing the growing unity among the seekers, tailored their teachings to strengthen the bonds forged in the cosmic dance. Guru Amara, with his celestial wisdom, spoke of the interconnectedness of all beings and the importance of unity in restoring balance to the astral realms. Yogini Surya, with her yogic teachings, emphasized the harmony that arose from shared spiritual practices.

Under the guidance of Rishi Varun, the seekers participated in group meditations that transcended individual boundaries. The astral energies, magnified by the collective intent, resonated with a harmonic frequency that echoed the unity of the seekers' spirits. The Ganges, with its sacred currents, witnessed the bonds strengthening among the seekers as they flowed together in the cosmic river of enlightenment.

During moments of reflection beneath the Himalayan peaks, the seekers shared their innermost revelations and fears. Aadi, once haunted by shadows, found solace in the support of Priya and Rajveer. Priya, with her scientific gaze now tempered by spiritual insight, marveled at the interconnected threads that bound the trio. Rajveer, the historian, recognized the echoes of ancient tales in their shared journey—a tale that transcended individual destinies.

The shared meditative states, the yogic practices, and the cosmic revelations became threads that wove the seekers into a tapestry of unity. A growing sense of purpose emerged—a purpose that transcended the individual quest for astral equilibrium. The urgency of astral imbalances, once a daunting challenge, now became a shared responsibility that bound the seekers in a covenant of cosmic harmony.

As the seekers stood together beneath the stars of Rishikesh, the artifact resonating with the collective energies of the group, a silent acknowledgment passed between them. The Himalayan peaks, veiled in mist and ancient wisdom, seemed to nod in approval as the seekers embraced the unity forged in the crucible of spiritual training.

The next phase of their journey awaited—a journey that would see the strengthened bonds among the seekers become a force that could restore balance to the astral realms. The mystic trainers, with eyes that held the depth of cosmic insight, recognized the significance of the unity unfolding in Rishikesh.

Aditya, Priya, and Rajveer, bound by purpose and destiny, stood ready to face the cosmic dance as a united front. The artifact, now infused with the collective energies of the trio, pulsed with a luminous glow that mirrored the bonds strengthened in the spiritual haven of Rishikesh. The unfolding chapters of "The Astral Chronicles" held the promise of a cosmic odyssey guided by the unity that had become the beating heart of their shared journey.

# Chapter 22: Astral Trials

**The trio faces astral trials, testing their newfound abilities.
Hints of a greater cosmic imbalance.**

In the sanctified realms of Rishikesh, where the Ganges whispered cosmic hymns and the Himalayan peaks stood as silent witnesses to ancient truths, Aditya "Aadi" Sharma, Priya Mehta, and Rajveer Kapoor faced a pivotal juncture in their spiritual journey. Guided by the mystic trainers and fortified by strengthened bonds, the trio embarked on astral trials that would test their newfound abilities and unveil hints of a greater cosmic imbalance.

As the seekers ventured into the astral realms, the Ganges' sacred currents mirrored the celestial energies that flowed through their consciousness. The artifact, pulsating with the collective powers of Aadi, Priya, and Rajveer, became a beacon that guided them through the cosmic currents of their trials. The mystic trainers, with their eyes holding the depth of cosmic insight, stood as guardians of the seekers' journey.

The first astral trial unfolded in the celestial expanse—a realm where constellations danced and astral gateways beckoned. Aadi, Priya, and Rajveer navigated the cosmic currents with a newfound unity, their abilities honed through the spiritual training in Rishikesh. The artifact, infused with celestial power, responded to their collective intent, marking a harmonious passage through the astral dance.

Yet, hints of a greater cosmic imbalance lingered. Shadows, more elusive than those in their inner realms, danced on the edges of the astral tapestry. The mystic trainers, attuned to the subtle shifts in cosmic energies, observed the trials with vigilant eyes. Guru Amara spoke of the interconnectedness of astral realms, warning of the delicate balance that teetered on the brink of disharmony.

The second trial led the seekers through the astral gateways—a journey that transcended the earthly confines and ventured into realms where celestial beings whispered cosmic truths. Aadi, guided by the artifact's resonance, projected his consciousness with greater control. Priya deciphered celestial patterns that hinted at the origins of the astral imbalances. Rajveer, with his historical perspective, recognized echoes of cosmic tales that spoke of a cosmic equilibrium under threat.

As the seekers traversed the astral gateways, a sense of urgency enveloped them. The artifact, now a conduit for their collective abilities, pulsed with a rhythm that echoed the cosmic heartbeat. The mystic trainers, with a shared understanding of the cosmic dance, hinted at the presence of an unseen force — a cosmic imbalance that transcended individual trials.

The third trial unfolded in the celestial convergence—a nexus where earthly and astral energies intertwined. Aadi, Priya, and Rajveer, their abilities refined through the preceding trials, stood at the threshold of cosmic revelation. The artifact, resonant with celestial power, hummed in anticipation as the seekers confronted the echoes of cosmic disharmony.

The mystic trainers, sensing the culmination of the astral trials, spoke of a greater purpose that awaited the seekers. The Ganges, with its sacred currents, whispered of a cosmic dance that transcended the earthly plane. The Himalayan peaks, veiled in mist and ancient wisdom, bore witness to the seekers' journey through the astral realms.

As the astral trials reached their zenith, the seekers glimpsed the magnitude of the cosmic imbalance—a force that threatened to disrupt the very fabric of the astral dance. Shadows, once elusive, coalesced into a looming presence that echoed the disharmony resonating in the cosmic currents.

Aditya, Priya, and Rajveer, now seasoned travelers of the astral realms, faced the daunting reality of a greater cosmic imbalance. The artifact, now a beacon infused with the collective energies of the trio, pulsed with a luminous intensity that marked the beginning of a cosmic odyssey with stakes higher than ever before.

The next chapters of "The Astral Chronicles" beckoned—the seekers, united by purpose and strengthened by bonds forged in Rishikesh, stood ready to confront the cosmic imbalance that threatened the astral realms. The mystic trainers, their eyes reflecting the cosmic truths hidden in the depths of the Ganges and the Himalayan peaks, guided the seekers toward a destiny woven into the celestial fabric of existence.

# Chapter 23: Celestial Council

**A vision leads the team to an encounter with celestial beings.**
**Insights into their mission and the impending astral challenge.**

In the ethereal glow of the astral nexus, the team found themselves drawn into a collective vision. The cosmic energies resonated with ancient echoes, revealing a celestial council—beings of light and wisdom who presided over the cosmic balance.

As the vision unfolded, the team stood in a celestial chamber adorned with luminescent constellations. The air shimmered with energies, and the celestial beings manifested before them in radiant forms. Their presence exuded a profound serenity, yet their eyes held the weight of cosmic responsibilities.

Aadi, Priya, Raj, and the rest of the team bowed respectfully as the celestial council acknowledged their presence. These celestial entities, guardians of astral realms, were adorned with celestial robes that mirrored the stars, and their features held the timeless wisdom of cosmic existence.

The leader of the council, a venerable being with eyes that held the depth of eternity, spoke with a voice that resonated through the very fabric of reality. "Champions of the mortal realms, you stand at the precipice of a cosmic challenge. The astral energies surge and the tapestry of destiny await your influence."

The vision seamlessly transitioned, revealing glimpses of their past endeavors, the threads of destiny woven through their actions, and the pivotal role they played in maintaining the delicate equilibrium between the mortal and astral worlds.

Aadi, guided by celestial intuition, felt a surge of cosmic energies intertwining with the threads of their fates. Priya, the empathic anchor, sensed the celestial beings' emotions—a blend of hope, concern, and unwavering resolve. Raj, embodiment of sacrifice, felt the weight of the impending astral challenge and the sacrifices it demanded.

The celestial council spoke, "You bear the celestial emblem—a mark of destiny that binds you to the astral realms. The nexus has chosen you to safeguard the cosmic balance. As champions, you shall navigate the cosmic currents and face trials that transcend mortal understanding."

Insights into the impending astral challenge unfolded—a cosmic convergence that threatened to disrupt the harmony between worlds. The team's mission became clear: to venture into the heart of the astral maelstrom, confront the shadows seeking ascendance, and restore the celestial accord.

The celestial beings bestowed upon each team member a cosmic blessing—a surge of energy that heightened their senses and attuned them to the astral forces. Aadi, Priya, Raj, and their comrades felt a celestial resonance within, an echo of the council's wisdom guiding them in the impending astral challenge.

With the vision fading, the celestial leader imparted a final message, "Champions, your journey is intertwined with the cosmic dance. Embrace your destinies, for the threads you weave, will echo through the realms. May the celestial accord guide and protect you in the trials that wait."

As the team returned to the nexus, the vision lingered—a celestial imprint on their consciousness, marking the beginning of a transformative chapter in their cosmic odyssey. The encounter with the celestial council fueled their determination, and the echoes of celestial wisdom propelled them toward the imminent astral challenge that waited beyond the veil.

# Chapter 24: Shadows Stirring

**A dark force becomes aware of the team's progress.**
**Ominous signs of ancient evils resurfacing.**

In the ethereal landscapes of the astral realms, where the cosmic dance unfolded with the rhythm of celestial energies, Aditya "Aadi" Sharma, Priya Mehta, and Rajveer Kapoor faced a formidable turning point in their journey. The astral trials had honed their abilities, and the bonds forged in Rishikesh strengthened their unity. However, amidst the harmonious currents, shadows stirred—a dark force became aware of the team's progress, and ominous signs hinted at ancient evils resurfacing.

As the seekers navigated the astral realms, the Ganges' sacred currents mirrored the heightened frequencies of their consciousness. The artifact, now pulsating with celestial power, guided Aadi, Priya, and Rajveer through the cosmic currents. The mystic trainers, guardians of the seekers' journey, sensed a disturbance in the astral tapestry—a presence that transcended the ordinary trials.

In the celestial expanse, shadows coalesced into a dark force—an entity that cast a malevolent gaze upon the seekers' progress. Guru Amara, with his celestial wisdom, spoke of ancient evils that lurked in the astral realms, drawn to the seekers' burgeoning powers. Yogini Surya and Rishi Varun, their eyes reflecting the Ganges' sacred waters, warned of a looming cosmic imbalance that echoed the ominous signs.

The artifact, resonant with celestial power, hummed in response to the cosmic disturbance. Aadi, Priya, and Rajveer, their astral abilities honed through trials and unity, sensed the encroaching shadows. The astral plane, once a canvas of cosmic wonders, now bore the marks of a dark force aware of the seekers' journey.

In the astral gateways, the ominous signs became more pronounced. Celestial patterns, once harmonious, shifted under the influence of the malevolent force. Aadi's astral projections, now a beacon in the astral realms, attracted the attention of unseen entities that whispered ancient incantations. Priya's astrophysical insights revealed celestial anomalies that mirrored the signs of impending darkness. Rajveer, the historian, recognized echoes of ancient tales foretelling the resurgence of cosmic evils.

The mystic trainers, their cosmic insight sharpened by centuries of wisdom, guided the seekers through the celestial convergence—the nexus where the ominous signs manifested with greater intensity. The Ganges, with its sacred currents, seemed to ripple with a disquiet that mirrored the cosmic imbalance. The Himalayan peaks, veiled in mist and ancient wisdom, echoed the whispers of a darkness that sought to engulf the astral realms.

As the shadows stirred in the astral realms, the seekers stood at the precipice of a cosmic confrontation. The artifact, now a conduit for the collective energies of Aadi, Priya, and Rajveer, pulsed with a luminous determination to confront the encroaching darkness. The mystic trainers, their gaze reflecting the cosmic truths hidden in the astral tapestry, prepared the seekers for a battle that transcended the earthly and astral planes.

The next chapters of "The Astral Chronicles" beckoned—the seekers, aware of the shadows stirring in the astral realms, prepared to face the ancient evils that sought to disrupt the cosmic dance. The artifact, infused with the unity of the trio and the wisdom of Rishikesh, stood as a beacon against the encroaching darkness. The Himalayan peaks, silent witnesses to cosmic destinies, awaited the seekers' resolve to confront the shadows that threatened to engulf the astral realms in an age-old battle between light and darkness.

# Chapter 25: Veiled Threats

**The team experiences confrontations with astral entities. Aadi's connection to the artifact becomes both strength and vulnerability.**

In the astral realms, where celestial energies interwove with the cosmic dance, Aditya "Aadi" Sharma, Priya Mehta, and Rajveer Kapoor faced a perilous chapter in their journey. The shadows, stirred by a malevolent force aware of the seekers' progress, manifested into veiled threats—confrontations with astral entities that tested the trio's resolve. Aadi's connection to the artifact, once a beacon of celestial power, became both strength and vulnerability as the veiled threats unfolded.

As the seekers traversed the astral realms, guided by the pulsating artifact, ominous entities materialized in the celestial expanse. The Ganges' sacred currents, usually a source of cosmic wisdom, seemed to ripple with an unsettling energy. The mystic trainers, with their eyes reflecting the astral tapestry, warned of veiled threats that sought to challenge the seekers' mastery.

The first confrontation occurred in the astral gateways—a realm where the veiled threats took shape as ethereal entities that mirrored the shadows of cosmic disharmony. Aadi, Priya, and Rajveer, united by purpose and strengthened by their bonds, faced the entities with determination. The artifact, resonant with celestial power, emitted a luminous glow that defied the encroaching darkness.

Aadi's mastery over astral projections became a beacon in the confrontations, guiding the seekers through the veiled threats with precision. However, the malevolent force, aware of Aadi's connection to the artifact, sought to exploit it as vulnerability. The artifact, now a conduit for the collective energies of the trio, echoed with the struggles of the astral confrontations.

In the celestial convergence, where the veiled threats intensified, Priya's astrophysical insights unveiled the entities' origin—a darkness that transcended the astral realms. Rajveer, with his historical perspective, recognized echoes of ancient tales describing astral entities bound by malevolent forces. The mystic trainers, their celestial wisdom ever-present, urged the seekers to delve deeper into the unity forged in Rishikesh.

Aadi, his connection to the artifact tested by the veiled threats, felt the weight of both strength and vulnerability. The artifact's luminous glow intensified as the seekers confronted the astral entities, but shadows danced on the edges, threatening to exploit the seams of Aadi's astral mastery.

As the veiled threats reached their zenith, the seekers stood at the crossroads of cosmic destinies. The Ganges, with its sacred currents, seemed to mirror the struggles of the astral confrontations. The Himalayan peaks, veiled in mist and ancient wisdom, watched over the seekers as they faced the malevolent force that sought to disrupt the celestial dance.

The next chapters of "The Astral Chronicles" beckoned—the seekers, united by purpose and fortified by their shared journey, prepared to confront the veiled threats that hinted at a cosmic imbalance. The artifact, now a symbol of both strength and vulnerability, pulsed with the collective energies of Aadi, Priya, and Rajveer. The mystic trainers, with their eyes, reflecting the cosmic truths hidden in the astral tapestry, guided the seekers toward a destiny that transcended the ordinary trials—a destiny where the veiled threats would be unveiled, and the shadows that stirred in the astral realms would face the luminous determination of those who sought to restore balance to the cosmic dance.

# Chapter 26: Varanasi's Echo

**The group returns to Varanasi, where shadows from the past await. Varanasi's mystic energies intensify.**

Back in the ancient city of Varanasi, where the Ganges flowed with the rhythm of cosmic currents and the echoes of millennia lingered in the air, Aditya "Aadi" Sharma, Priya Mehta, and Rajveer Kapoor returned to confront shadows from the past. The veiled threats faced in the astral realms had drawn them back to the place where their journey had begun. Varanasi's mystic energies, intensified by the unfolding cosmic drama, awaited the seekers with a resonance that transcended the ordinary.

As the seekers stepped onto the sacred Ghats of Varanasi, the Ganges seemed to whisper ancient tales, carrying the echoes of astral confrontations and cosmic imbalances. The artifact, pulsating with the collective energies of Aadi, Priya, and Rajveer, resonated with a luminous intensity that marked their return to the city where dormant powers had been awakened.

Shadows from the past awaited the seekers in Varanasi—whispers of ancient evils and astral entities that had been veiled by the currents of time. Guru Amara's celestial wisdom, gained in Rishikesh, echoed in the seekers' consciousness as they confronted the shadows that stirred along the banks of the Ganges.

The mystic trainers, their eyes reflecting the cosmic truths hidden in the astral tapestry, guided the seekers toward the heart of Varanasi's mystic energies. Yogini Surya and Rishi Varun, their essence attuned to the celestial currents, sensed the intensified resonance that marked Varanasi's echo in the cosmic dance.

The first confrontation unfolded at the ancient temples of Varanasi—a sacred nexus where earthly and astral energies converged. The veiled threats, once ethereal in the astral realms, manifested as shadows clinging to the ancient stones. Aadi, Priya, and Rajveer, fortified by their experiences and unity, faced the shadows with a determination that echoed the luminous glow of the artifact.

Varanasi's mystic energies intensified—the sacred waters of the Ganges carried the seekers through a cosmic dance that mirrored the astral confrontations. The artifact, now a symbol of resilience, hummed with the echoes of ancient truths that transcended the ordinary boundaries of time.

In the heart of Varanasi, where the past and present intertwined, the seekers confronted the shadows that stirred along the Ghats. Aadi's connection to the artifact, once both strength and vulnerability, now became a beacon that illuminated the shadows with celestial power. The mystic trainers, with their celestial insight, spoke of Varanasi's echo—a resonance that held the key to unraveling the cosmic imbalance.

As the seekers delved deeper into Varanasi's mystic energies, they uncovered ancient inscriptions and symbols that spoke of cosmic battles fought in epochs long past. The Ganges, with its sacred currents, whispered the secrets of Varanasi's echo—a resonance that transcended mortal understanding. The Himalayan peaks, veiled in mist and ancient wisdom, seemed to nod in acknowledgment as the seekers confronted the shadows that lingered in the city's timeless embrace.

The next chapters of "The Astral Chronicles" beckoned—the seekers now returned to Varanasi, stood at the intersection of ancient tales and cosmic revelations. The artifact, resonant with the luminous determination of Aadi, Priya, and Rajveer, pulsed with a celestial energy that echoed Varanasi's mystic echo. The Himalayan peaks, silent witnesses to cosmic destinies, awaited the seekers' resolve to confront the shadows that stirred along the Ghats—a confrontation that would unveil the truths hidden within Varanasi's ancient embrace.

# Chapter 27: Dance of Light and Shadow

**Aadi faces a personal astral confrontation.**
**Raj reveals his martial arts expertise in protecting the team.**

In the sacred embrace of Varanasi, where the Ganges whispered cosmic hymns and the ancient stones bore witness to the echoes of time, Aditya "Aadi" Sharma faced a personal astral confrontation. Shadows stirred within the depths of his consciousness, echoing the dance of light and shadow that unfolded along the ghats. As Aadi grappled with the veiled threats within, Rajveer Kapoor revealed a facet of his expertise, showcasing martial arts prowess to protect the team in the midst of Varanasi's mystical energies.

The personal astral confrontation unfolded for Aadi beneath the cosmic canopy of Varanasi's night sky. The artifact, pulsating with celestial power, became a focal point for Aadi's astral projections. The shadows from his past, now given form in the astral realms, challenged him with echoes of doubt and unresolved fears.

Guru Amara's celestial wisdom, gained in Rishikesh, resonated within Aadi's consciousness. The mystic trainers, their eyes reflecting the cosmic truths hidden in the astral tapestry, observed the dance of light and shadow that unfolded within the seeker's inner realms.

As Aadi confronted the veiled threats within, the Ganges' sacred currents seemed to mirror the astral turbulence. The artifact, infused with the luminous determination of the seekers, emitted a glow that transcended the earthly plane. The Himalayan peaks, veiled in mist and ancient wisdom, stood as silent witnesses to Aadi's astral journey—a journey that echoed the cosmic dance unfolding along the Ghats.

75

Meanwhile, on the earthly plane, Rajveer Kapoor revealed his martial arts expertise. Varanasi's mystic energies, intensified by the unfolding cosmic drama, had drawn the attention of tangible threats. Shadows that stirred along the Ghats materialized into adversaries seeking to disrupt the seekers' journey.

Raj, with fluid grace and precision, moved like a dance of light amidst the shadows. His martial arts prowess became a shield that protected the seekers from the tangible threats that sought to encroach upon Varanasi's mystical embrace. The artifact, resonant with celestial power, pulsed in tandem with the dance of light and shadow on the earthly plane.

As Aadi delved deeper into his personal astral confrontation, Raj's martial arts expertise became a vital force in maintaining the harmony of the cosmic dance. The ancient stones of Varanasi, imbued with the echoes of countless tales, bore witness to the convergence of astral and earthly battles.

In the celestial convergence of Varanasi's energies, Aadi's astral projections confronted the shadows within with unwavering determination. The dance of light and shadow, both personal and tangible, echoed along the Ghats—a reflection of the cosmic balance that hung in the delicate equilibrium.

The next chapters of "The Astral Chronicles" beckoned—the seekers, unified by purpose and fortified by their unique strengths, stood ready to face the shadows that lingered within and outside Varanasi's mystical embrace. The artifact, pulsating with the luminous determination of Aadi, Priya, and Rajveer, became a symbol of resilience in the dance of light and shadow that transcended the boundaries of the earthly and astral realms. The Himalayan peaks, guardians of cosmic destinies, awaited the seekers' resolve to navigate the intricate steps of the cosmic dance—a dance that echoed in the celestial convergence of Varanasi's timeless nights.

# Chapter 28: Guardian Unveiled

**Mira Devi, a mysterious guardian, appears, offering guidance. The team learns of a prophecy involving their intertwined fates.**

Amidst the mystical energies of Varanasi, where the Ganges flowed with the wisdom of epochs and the ancient stones whispered cosmic secrets, a new chapter unfolded in the cosmic odyssey of Aditya "Aadi" Sharma, Priya Mehta, and Rajveer Kapoor. As the seekers grappled with personal astral confrontations and the dance of light and shadow, a mysterious guardian emerged—Mira Devi, offering guidance that would unveil a prophecy involving the intertwined fates of the team.

Beneath the celestial canopy of Varanasi's night sky, Mira Devi appeared—a luminous figure with eyes that held the depth of cosmic insight. The artifact, pulsating with celestial power, seemed to resonate in harmony with her presence. The mystic trainers, their gaze reflecting the astral tapestry, acknowledged the arrival of a guardian whose role in the cosmic dance held the key to unraveling the seekers' destinies.

Mira Devi, with a voice that echoed like the sacred currents of the Ganges, spoke of ancient prophecies that bound the seekers together. The dance of light and shadow, the personal astral confrontations, and Rajveer's martial prowess—all were threads woven into a cosmic tapestry that foretold a destiny beyond the ordinary realms.

In the celestial convergence of Varanasi's energies, Mira Devi guided the seekers through the veiled threats and shadows that lingered along the Ghats. Her presence, like a beacon of celestial guidance, illuminated the path that the seekers were destined to tread. The artifact, now infused with the collective energies of Aadi, Priya, and Rajveer, pulsed with a luminosity that mirrored the unfolding prophecy.

As Mira Devi spoke, the Ganges' sacred currents seemed to whisper tales of an age-old prophecy involving the seekers' intertwined fates. The mystic trainers, their celestial wisdom deepened by the guardian's presence, acknowledged the significance of the cosmic dance that had brought Aadi, Priya, and Rajveer together.

The prophecy spoke of a cosmic imbalance that threatened the very fabric of the astral realms. Aadi's connection to the artifact, Priya's astrophysical insights, Rajveer's martial prowess, and the unity forged in Rishikesh—all were threads woven into a tapestry that held the power to restore balance to the cosmic dance.

Mira Devi, with her luminous presence, became a guide in the seekers' journey—a guardian unveiled to illuminate the path that transcended the ordinary boundaries of time and space. The artifact, now resonant with the celestial guidance, pulsed with a rhythm that echoed the cosmic dance of destinies.

The next chapters of "The Astral Chronicles" beckoned—the seekers, now aware of the prophecy that bound their fates, prepared to face the challenges that waited in the astral realms. Mira Devi, with eyes that held the depth of cosmic insight, guided Aadi, Priya, and Rajveer toward a destiny that would see them confront the shadows that stirred along the Ghats and unravel the cosmic imbalance that threatened the astral tapestry. The Himalayan peaks, silent witnesses to cosmic destinies, waited the unfolding of the prophecy that would guide the seekers toward the heart of the celestial dance.

# Chapter 29: Ties That Bind

**A deeper understanding of the characters' interconnected pasts.
The team realizes their destinies are intricately linked.**

In the ancient city of Varanasi, where the Ganges whispered cosmic hymns and the shadows of destiny danced along the Ghats, a pivotal chapter unfolded in the cosmic odyssey of Aditya "Aadi" Sharma, Priya Mehta, and Rajveer Kapoor. Guided by the mysterious guardian Mira Devi, the seekers delved into the depths of their interconnected pasts, discovering ties that bound their destinies in ways they had never imagined.

As the seekers stood beneath the celestial canopy, Mira Devi's luminous presence illuminated the ancient stones that bore witness to the unfolding cosmic drama. The artifact, resonant with celestial power, seemed to vibrate with a rhythm that echoed the ties that bound the seekers together. The mystic trainers, their celestial gaze penetrating the veil of time, acknowledged the significance of the journey that had brought Aadi, Priya, and Rajveer together.

Mira Devi began to unravel the threads of the past—a tapestry woven with echoes of ancient tales and cosmic destinies. Aadi's charismatic archaeologist persona hid the lineage of ancient mystics, his family connected to the very artifact that now pulsed with celestial power. Priya, the astrophysicist with a scientific gaze, traced her ancestry to seers who had deciphered celestial patterns since time immemorial. Rajveer, the martial arts expert and historian, carried within him the echoes of warriors who had guarded the astral realms through the ages.

The Ganges, with its sacred currents, whispered tales of the seekers' intertwined pasts—a narrative that transcended individual stories and flowed as a collective cosmic stream. The artifact, now a conduit for the seekers' destinies, hummed with the resonance of ties that bound Aadi, Priya, and Rajveer in a dance that spanned epochs.

As Mira Devi spoke, the seekers glimpsed visions of their ancestors—figures from ancient times who had stood at the crossroads of cosmic destinies. The dance of light and shadow, the astral trials, and the veiled threats—all were revealed as echoes of a cosmic drama that had played out in the tapestry of time.

In the celestial convergence of Varanasi's energies, the seekers realized the intricacies of their destinies. Aadi's connection to the artifact, Priya's astrophysical insights, and Rajveer's martial prowess were not mere happenstance. The threads of their pasts, woven into the cosmic tapestry, created a harmony that held the power to restore balance to the astral realms.

The ties that bound the seekers went beyond the earthly plane—they transcended mortal understanding and resonated with the cosmic dance. Mira Devi, with her celestial guidance, became a guardian who had waited through the ages for the seekers to unite and fulfill the prophecy that held the key to the astral balance.

As the realization of their interconnected pasts settled within the seekers' consciousness, a sense of purpose emerged. The artifact, infused with the luminous determination of Aadi, Priya, and Rajveer, pulsed with celestial energy that mirrored the ties that bound the trio in a cosmic dance of destinies.

The next chapters of "The Astral Chronicles" beckoned—the seekers, now aware of the intricate ties that bound their destinies, prepared to confront the shadows along the Ghats and unravel the cosmic imbalance that threatened the astral tapestry. The Himalayan peaks, silent witnesses to the cosmic drama, awaited the seekers' resolve to navigate the intricacies of the celestial dance—a dance where the ties that bound them would be the very threads that wove the destiny of the astral realms.

# Chapter 30: Shadows Ascendant

**A dark force unleashes astral minions, intensifying the impending cosmic imbalance.**
**The team must prepare for an imminent showdown.**

In the ancient city of Varanasi, where the Ganges murmured cosmic hymns and the seekers had unveiled the ties that intricately bound their destinies, a looming Chapter unfurled in the cosmic journey of Aditya "Aadi" Sharma, Priya Mehta, and Rajveer Kapoor. As the echoes of interconnected pasts lingered in the air, a malevolent force ascended, releasing astral minions that intensified the impending cosmic imbalance. The team, guided by the mysterious guardian Mira Devi, teetered on the brink of an imminent showdown against shadows threatening to disrupt the delicate dance of astral realms.

The night sky above Varanasi bore witness to the rise of shadows—a dark force that harnessed astral minions to amplify the cosmic imbalance. The artifact, pulsating with the collective energies of Aadi, Priya, and Rajveer, hummed urgently, mirroring the looming threat. The mystic trainers, their celestial gaze intensified, warned of the shadows ascending with a darkness surpassing the ordinary bounds of the astral realms.

Mira Devi, the guardian with eyes reflecting cosmic depths, spoke of an ancient adversary—the very force that sought to disrupt the cosmic dance since time immemorial. The ties that bound the seekers now became a target for the shadows ascendant, each thread of destiny a focal point for the malevolent force seeking to tip the astral balance.

The Ganges, with its sacred currents, whispered tales of ancient battles fought along the Ghats. The mystic trainers, armed with celestial wisdom, urged the seekers to prepare for the imminent showdown against the shadows ascending in Varanasi's mystical embrace.

Aadi, Priya, and Rajveer fortified themselves, drawing upon the unity forged in Rishikesh and the knowledge gained on their journey. The personal astral confrontations, the dance of light and shadow, and the realization of interconnected pasts—all were stepping stones leading to this pivotal moment.

The shadows ascendant manifested as astral minions—ethereal entities that lurked along the Ghats, their malevolent presence casting a pall over the cosmic dance. The artifact, now a beacon of resilience, emitted a luminosity that stood in stark contrast to the encroaching darkness.

In the celestial convergence of Varanasi's energies, the team prepared for the imminent showdown. Mira Devi, with her celestial guidance, spoke of a ritual that could seal the shadows and restore balance to the astral realms. The artifact, resonant with the unity of the seekers, pulsed with a determination echoing the resolve to confront the ascendant shadows.

As the night deepened, the astral minions intensified their presence, dancing along the Ghats in a sinister choreography. The seekers, their destinies intertwined and fortified by the ties that bound them, stood ready to face the shadows in a cosmic showdown that would determine the fate of the astral realms.

The next chapters of "The Astral Chronicles" beckoned—the seekers, guided by Mira Devi and armed with the artifact's celestial power, prepared to confront the shadows that ascended in Varanasi. The Himalayan peaks, silent witnesses to cosmic destinies, awaited the resolution of the imminent showdown—a showdown that would echo through the astral realms and decide whether the dance of light or the shadows would prevail in the delicate balance of existence.

# Chapter 31: Celestial Intervention

**Celestial beings provide the team with ancient artifacts.**
**The artifacts enhance their abilities for the final confrontation.**

As the shadows ascendant cast an ominous veil over Varanasi, the seekers, Aditya "Aadi" Sharma, Priya Mehta, and Rajveer Kapoor, stood poised at the precipice of a cosmic showdown. In the stillness of the night, celestial beings descended, drawn by the imminent threat that threatened to disrupt the delicate dance of astral realms. With ethereal grace, these otherworldly entities bestowed upon the team ancient artifacts, enhancing their abilities for the final confrontation against the shadows that loomed.

The celestial intervention unfolded under the gaze of the guardian, Mira Devi, whose eyes reflected recognition as the celestial beings approached. Each being radiated an otherworldly luminosity, their presence resonating with the cosmic currents that flowed through Varanasi. The Ganges, with sacred currents hushed in anticipation, seemed to bow to the celestial intervention.

The artifacts, handed to Aadi, Priya, and Rajveer, pulsed with celestial energies that harmonized with the artifacts already in their possession. The ethereal gifts resonated with the seekers' destinies, each artifact a key to unlocking latent potential and fortifying their unity against the impending cosmic imbalance.

As the celestial beings bestowed the artifacts, a surge of celestial power flowed through the seekers. Aadi's connection to the artifact deepened, Priya's astrophysical insights became more profound, and Rajveer's martial prowess received a celestial augmentation. The artifacts, now a fusion of ancient and celestial energies, emitted a harmonious glow that permeated the mystical ambiance of Varanasi.

The mystic trainers, their celestial wisdom attuned to the unfolding drama, acknowledged the significance of the celestial intervention. Mira Devi, with a nod of gratitude, recognized the artifacts as keys to unlocking the seekers' true potential—a potential that transcended mortal limits and mirrored the celestial dance of the astral realms.

The celestial beings, with their otherworldly presence, spoke of a cosmic synergy that bound the seekers and the artifacts. The Ganges, with its sacred currents, seemed to carry whispers of ancient alliances forged between celestial entities and earthly guardians. The artifacts, now enhanced by celestial intervention, resonated in harmony with the Ganges' cosmic hymns.

As the seekers held their newly bestowed artifacts, the celestial beings ascended, leaving behind a shimmering trail of stardust that mingled with the sacred currents of the Ganges. The night sky, now adorned with the luminosity of celestial gifts, reflected the impending confrontation against the shadows ascendant.

In the celestial convergence of Varanasi's energies, the seekers felt the enhanced resonance of their abilities. The artifacts, pulsating with celestial power, became conduits for the unity of Aadi, Priya, and Rajveer. The looming shadows, sensing the celestial intervention, quivered in anticipation of the cosmic showdown that waited.

The next chapters of "The Astral Chronicles" beckoned—the seekers, armed with artifacts bestowed by celestial beings, prepared to face the shadows that ascended in Varanasi. The Himalayan peaks, silent witnesses to cosmic destinies, awaited the resolution of the imminent showdown—a showdown where the celestial intervention would be the key to tipping the delicate balance of the astral dance in favor of the seekers and the cosmic realms they sought to protect.

# Chapter 32: The Astral Showdown

**A climactic battle against astral forces in Varanasi.**
**The team faces personal challenges and revelations.**

U nder the cloak of night in Varanasi, the sacred city echoed with the anticipation of a cosmic confrontation. Aadi Sharma, Priya Mehta, and Rajveer Kapoor, armed with artifacts bestowed by celestial beings, stood at the threshold of the astral showdown against the shadows ascendant. The Ganges whispered cosmic hymns, and the ancient stones bore witness to the climactic battle that would decide the fate of the astral realms.

As the seekers approached the Ghats, the shadows ascendant manifested into astral forces—an ethereal army that danced along the riverbanks, their malevolent presence casting a pall over Varanasi's mystical ambiance. The artifacts, pulsating with celestial power, resonated in tandem with the looming shadows, creating a cosmic symphony that reverberated through the astral realms.

The guardian, Mira Devi, stood at the forefront, her luminous presence illuminating the path that led to the heart of the astral showdown. The mystic trainers, with celestial insight, guided the seekers, their gaze reflecting the cosmic truths hidden within the astral tapestry.

The artifacts, now enhanced by celestial intervention, became conduits for the seekers' abilities. Aadi, with his connection to the artifact, felt the surge of celestial energy coursing through his veins. Priya, attuned to astrophysical insights, glimpsed patterns in the astral dance that were invisible to mortal eyes. Rajveer, his martial prowess augmented by celestial grace, moved with a fluidity that transcended earthly limits.

As the climactic battle unfolded, the seekers faced personal challenges—echoes of their pasts materializing as astral trials. Aadi confronted shadows that mirrored his inner doubts, Priya deciphered celestial patterns that held glimpses of her ancestral seers, and Rajveer faced adversaries that tested the limits of his martial prowess.

The Ganges, with sacred currents flowing as an ethereal battleground, reflected the cosmic drama that played out along its banks. The artifact, resonant with the unity of the seekers, emitted a luminosity that rivaled the shadows' malevolence. The celestial beings, their influence lingering in the artifacts, watched as the astral showdown unfolded—a dance of light and shadow that decided the fate of the astral realms.

Revelations emerged amidst the chaos—a celestial prophecy echoed in the clashes, personal trials unraveled cosmic truths, and the shadows ascendant, faced with the seekers' celestial power, quivered with a realization that their malevolence could not endure the unity of the trio.

In the celestial convergence of Varanasi's energies, the seekers confronted the shadows with unwavering determination. The artifacts, pulsating with celestial power, became instruments of the cosmic dance—a dance that transcended earthly boundaries and mirrored the delicate balance of the astral realms.

As the astral forces clashed, the seekers' unity deepened. Aadi, Priya, and Rajveer, their destinies intertwined and fortified by the celestial gifts, stood as guardians of the astral realms. The Ganges, with sacred currents singing hymns of cosmic victory, witnessed the culmination of the showdown.

The next chapters of "The Astral Chronicles" beckoned—the seekers, now victors in the astral showdown, faced the aftermath of the climactic battle. The artifacts, still resonant with celestial power, held the key to restoring balance to the astral realms. The Himalayan peaks, silent witnesses to cosmic destinies, awaited the seekers' resolve as they navigated the aftermath of the astral showdown—a resolution that would echo through the astral tapestry and shape the destiny of the seekers and the realms they sought to protect.

# Chapter 33: Balancing Act

**The trio succeeds in restoring a temporary balance.**
**Hints of a greater cosmic quest yet to unfold.**

In the aftermath of the astral showdown along the sacred banks of Varanasi, Aadi Sharma, Priya Mehta, and Rajveer Kapoor stood amidst the lingering echoes of celestial confrontation. The astral forces, once ascendant, now quivered in the wake of the seekers' victory, and the Ganges flowed with a renewed serenity. Guided by the artifacts bestowed by celestial beings, the trio embarked on a delicate balancing act, seeking to restore temporary harmony to the astral realms.

The artifacts, pulsating with the residual energy of the astral showdown, emitted a luminosity that reflected the unity of Aadi, Priya, and Rajveer. The guardian, Mira Devi, acknowledged the seekers' success in the balancing acts—a testament to their resilience and celestial grace.

As the seekers performed a ritual along the Ghats, the artifacts became conduits for restoring balance to the astral realms. The Ganges, with sacred currents now harmonized, whispered cosmic hymns that resonated with the seekers' celestial journey. The mystic trainers, their celestial gaze contemplative, observed the delicate dance of energies as the trio worked to mend the astral tapestry.

Hints of a greater cosmic quest yet to unfold lingered in the air. The Ganges, with its timeless wisdom, carried whispers of ancient prophecies that spoke of destinies entwined with celestial threads. The artifacts, still resonant with the celestial power, hinted at a purpose that transcended the recent astral showdown—a purpose that beckoned the seekers toward a greater cosmic quest.

In the celestial convergence of Varanasi's energies, the trio succeeded in the balancing act. The shadows, once ascendant, now retreated into the astral realms, their malevolence temporarily held at bay. The artifacts, with their celestial glow, stood as beacons of hope in the delicate balance the seekers had restored.

As the night embraced Varanasi, the seekers contemplated the aftermath of the astral showdown. The artifacts, now symbols of the trio's triumph, held the key to unlocking a cosmic quest that waited on the horizon. The Ganges, with its sacred currents, seemed to murmur tales of a journey yet to unfold—a journey that would echo through the astral tapestry and shape the destiny of Aadi, Priya, and Rajveer.

The next chapters of "The Astral Chronicles" beckoned—the seekers, now guardians of the temporary balance restored in Varanasi, prepared to embark on the greater cosmic quest hinted at by ancient prophecies. The artifacts, still infused with celestial power, became guides in the seekers' journey toward a destiny that waited beyond the familiar realms. The Himalayan peaks, silent witnesses to cosmic destinies, stood vigilant as the trio embraced the unfolding chapters of their celestial odyssey—a journey where the delicate balancing act would be but a prelude to the cosmic dance that awaited them in the vast expanse of the astral realms.

# Chapter 34: Aftermath

**The team reflects on their journey and the challenges ahead.**
**Mira Devi hints at the larger role they play in cosmic harmony.**

In the quiet aftermath of the astral showdown along the revered Ghats of Varanasi, Aadi Sharma, Priya Mehta, and Rajveer Kapoor stood amidst the echoes of celestial triumph. The artifacts, still resonant with the energies of their recent balancing act, held a quiet glow in the moonlit night. As the seekers gazed upon the Ganges, now flowing with a renewed serenity, they reflected on the journey that brought them to this pivotal moment.

Seated along the riverbank, the trio exchanged glances, each harboring the weight of the challenges faced and the revelations uncovered. The artifacts, once wielded in a cosmic battle, now rested in the hands of their guardians, pulsating with a celestial rhythm that mirrored the unity forged through trials and triumphs.

Mira Devi, the guardian with eyes reflecting the cosmic depths, joined the seekers on the riverbank. In the silent exchange of glances, she conveyed a wisdom that transcended mortal understanding. The guardian, attuned to the celestial currents, spoke of the delicate balancing act they had achieved—a testament to the seekers resilience and the celestial grace bestowed upon them.

The mystic trainers, with their celestial insight, acknowledged the significance of the seekers' journey—the dance of light and shadow, the astral trials, and the balancing act. The artifacts, now symbols of the seekers' victory, became focal points in the cosmic tapestry that wove together destinies and cosmic threads.

As the seekers took a moment to absorb the tranquility of the night, Mira Devi hinted at the larger role they played in the cosmic harmony. The Ganges, with its sacred currents, seemed to sing tales of a cosmic quest that awaited the trio. The artifacts, infused with celestial power, whispered of a purpose that transcended the recent astral showdown.

The guardian spoke of prophecies etched in the stars—of destinies entwined with the very fabric of the astral realms. Aadi, Priya, and Rajveer, now guardians of the delicate balance restored in Varanasi, were beckoned toward a greater cosmic quest. The Himalayan peaks, shrouded in the mysteries of ages, stood as silent witnesses to the unfolding destinies that echoed through the astral tapestry.

In the celestial convergence of Varanasi's energies, the seekers contemplated the challenges that lay ahead. The artifacts, still glowing with a celestial luminescence, guided their gaze toward the vast expanse of the astral realms—a canvas waiting to be painted with the strokes of their cosmic journey.

The next chapters of "The Astral Chronicles" beckoned—the seekers, now aware of their larger role in cosmic harmony, prepared to embark on the greater quest hinted at by prophecies and celestial insights. The artifacts, held with reverence, became tools in the seekers' hands as they stepped into the unknown realms that waited beyond the familiar horizons. The Ganges, with its sacred currents, seemed to bless the seekers, and the Himalayan peaks, guardians of ancient wisdom, stood resolute as the trio embraced the unfolding cosmic odyssey—a journey where the aftermath of the astral showdown was but a prelude to the mysteries that awaited in the cosmic dance of destinies.

# Chapter 35: Departure and Destiny

**The trio sets out on a new journey, realizing their destiny is intertwined with the astral realms.**
**The stage is set for the next installment of "The Astral Chronicles."**

Under the silvered canopy of Varanasi's night sky, Aadi Sharma, Priya Mehta, and Rajveer Kapoor prepared to depart from the sacred city, their destinies now intricately woven into the astral realms. The artifacts, held with reverence, pulsed with the celestial energy that had guided the seekers through trials and triumphs. The Ganges, with sacred currents carrying whispers of cosmic hymns, seemed to bid farewell as the seekers embarked on a new journey.

Mira Devi, the guardian with eyes reflecting cosmic depths, stood alongside the trio. In the silent exchange of glances, she conveyed a wisdom that hinted at the vastness of the astral realms and the role the seekers were destined to play. The mystic trainers, with their celestial insight, acknowledged the seekers' departure as a prelude to the cosmic dance that awaited them.

As the seekers boarded a boat along the Ganges, the artifacts resonated with a harmonious glow, echoing the unity of Aadi, Priya, and Rajveer. The guardian spoke of prophecies that whispered of a greater purpose—a purpose that would unfold in the vast expanse of the astral realms.

The Ganges, with its timeless wisdom, seemed to carry tales of cosmic quests and celestial odysseys. The artifacts, now symbols of the seekers' journey, glowed with the anticipation of the unknown. The Himalayan peaks, standing as silent sentinels, witnessed the trio's departure as they ventured into the realms that waited beyond the familiar horizons.

As the boat sailed along the sacred river, Mira Devi hinted at the cosmic dance that awaited the seekers. Aadi, Priya, and Rajveer, now guardians of the astral realms understood that their destinies were intertwined with the cosmic tapestry—a tapestry woven with threads of light and shadow, trials and triumphs.

The artifacts, held aloft by the seekers, became beacons guiding them toward the next chapter of their celestial odyssey. The Ganges, with its sacred currents, murmured cosmic lullabies, and the artifacts resonated with the heartbeat of the astral realms. The guardian's words echoed in the seekers' hearts as they set out on a journey where the familiar would blend with the extraordinary, and destinies would unfold against the backdrop of celestial mysteries.

The next chapters of "The Astral Chronicles" beckoned—the seekers, now aware of their destiny intricately entwined with the astral realms, prepared to embrace the cosmic dance that awaited them. The artifacts, still infused with celestial power, were instruments in the seekers' hands as they stepped into the vast expanse of the unknown—a departure that marked not an end, but a continuation of the cosmic tapestry. The Ganges, with sacred currents flowing in cosmic rhythm, blessed the seekers, and the Himalayan peaks, guardians of ancient secrets, stood sentinel as the trio embarked on the next installment of their celestial odyssey—a journey where departure and destiny merged in the unfolding cosmic dance of "The Astral Chronicles." Now we will meet together in the beautiful journey of our Hero's in next Book 2: "Celestial Convergence" Aadi joins forces with astrophysicist Priya Mehta and martial artist Rajveer "Raj" Kapoor to decode celestial prophecies in Hampi.

# Note to All our Readers and valuable the General Public

We hold steadfastly to the principles of transparency, integrity, and a genuine commitment to education. The intention behind our work is driven by a sincere desire to enlighten and inform, with absolutely no intention to harm or offend anyone in any way regarding the topics discussed in this eBook, as outlined above.

We want to clarify that our eBook is a result of creative input and on imaginary basis and research, and we have not sourced or attempted to replicate content from any external websites, applications, or publications. The content you find here has been generated using the Chat GPT Software and AI Software, and our aim is to provide you with valuable insights and knowledge.

We extend our heartfelt gratitude to you for choosing to engage with our work. Your cooperation and support are deeply appreciated. Your input is invaluable as we strive to continually improve and offer content that serves your interests and needs.

Thank you for being a part of our journey towards greater understanding and enlightenment.

Warm regards,

[ANANT RAM]

Author of *The Book series in 12 is titled "The Astral Chronicles: Book 1 –*

*Awakening Shadows"*

Please feel free to contact as for any suggestions and quarry at:

anantramboss1@gmail.com

# Don't miss out!

Visit the website below and you can sign up to receive emails whenever ANANT RAM BOSS publishes a new book. There's no charge and no obligation.

https://books2read.com/r/B-A-GGLBB-HMISC

**BOOKS 2 READ**

Connecting independent readers to independent writers.

Did you love *Awakening Shadows*? Then you should read *The Chronicles of Alarion- Part-1 "Alarion and the Key of Kallindor"*[1] by ANANT RAM!

In the opening installment of "The Chronicles of Alarion," we are introduced to Alarion, a seemingly ordinary young man living in the mundane world. Alarion's life takes a dramatic turn when he stumbles upon a mysterious and ornate key – the Key of Kallindor. This key, with its intricate and mystical design, is far from ordinary. It carries with it the power to unlock a hidden portal into a world of magic and wonder.

As Alarion unwittingly turns the key, he is transported into a realm unknown to most mortals. This is a place where magic flows like a river, mythical creatures roam, and the very air crackles with enchantment.

---

1. https://books2read.com/u/3kD0pg

2. https://books2read.com/u/3kD0pg

Alarion's introduction to this magical world is marked by both awe and trepidation.

Soon, he realizes that the Key of Kallindor is not merely a portal opener; it is a powerful artifact that holds the secrets of this realm. Alarion's journey, filled with curiosity and courage, begins as he seeks to unravel the mysteries of this new and enchanted land. Along the way, he encounters strange beings, makes new friends, and becomes embroiled in a quest that will forever alter the course of his life.

"Alarion and the Key of Kallindor" is a tale of transformation, discovery, and the commencement of a grand adventure. It lays the foundation for a hero's journey that will span seven books, each revealing new layers of magic, destiny, and courage in the face of ever-increasing challenges.

# Also by ANANT RAM BOSS

**1**
The Chronicles of Alarion -Part-6 "Alarion and the Nexus of Netheron"
"The Chronicles of Alarion -Part-7-"Alarion and the Legacy of Luminarya"

**The Astral Chronicles**
Awakening Shadows
Awakening Shadows

**Standalone**
Love's Delectable Harmony

# About the Author

Anant Ram Boss is an accomplished author with a passion for creating immersive worlds and captivating stories. His journey into the realm of writing began at an early age when he discovered the magic of words and the power of storytelling. Anant's dedication to his craft and his relentless pursuit of literary excellence have made him a notable figure in the world of fantasy literature.

With an imaginative mind that knows no bounds, Anant has the ability to transport readers to enchanting and mysterious realms. His writing is known for its vivid descriptions, well-drawn characters, and intricate plots that keep readers eagerly turning pages. He has an innate talent for weaving intricate tales filled with magic, adventure, and profound themes.

Throughout his career, Anant has received acclaim for his ability to craft epic sagas and captivating series that resonate with readers of all ages. The Sries, in particular, has garnered a devoted following, and it showcases Anant's mastery of the fantasy genre.

When he's not lost in the worlds he creates, Anant enjoys exploring the great outdoors, indulging in his love for photography, and seeking inspiration from the beauty of the natural world. His appreciation for nature often finds its way into his storytelling, enriching his narratives with a deep connection to the environment and the magic that exists within it.

Anant Ram Boss is not only a storyteller but also a world-builder, a dreamer, and an explorer of the human experience through the lens of fantasy literature. With each new book he writes, he invites readers to embark on journeys of the imagination, fostering a love for the magical and the wondrous that resides within us all.

Printed by Libri Plureos GmbH in Hamburg,
Germany

9 798223 691891